MONSTER

SHIGERU BRODY

Other Titles by Shigeru Brody

Titanoboa

Sea Creature

BASED ON A
TRUE STORY

February 22nd, 1941

Will Curtis wasn't quite certain he would survive the next five minutes.

The room was dingy, but not dark. It was hard to find dark rooms in downtown Los Angeles. But the place stunk of urine and vomit from the drunks. He guessed you couldn't have anything valuable there because it'd be stolen in a matter of minutes. And, the worst part, some of the biggest cockroaches he'd ever seen were crawling around like they owned the place.

He glanced down and saw one scurrying by his feet. He took a step back, though tried to do it as smoothly as possible so no one else would notice.

The two other men in the room, Russians he guessed, ran their hands over the Kg m/40 light machine gun that was laid out on the bed like it was a sexy wife waiting for her husband. A Swedish weapon that wasn't even available on the market yet; a bit rough around the edges. But boy did it sure as hell look like a million bucks, Will thought. Long and thin, but sturdy enough to let you know you were holding a serious gun.

"So we got ourselves a deal, fellas?" he said.

The Russians were tall men. One of them, the older one that seemed to be in charge, was examining the weapon up close. Looking down the barrel, running his fingers over of the trigger, holding the weapon up flat in the palm of his hand to test its balance. The other Russian, a portly man with a cigarette dangling from his mouth, eyed the weapon close and then lost interest. He was now staring out the window at the street two stories below. A woman in a skirt was walking by, and his eyes were glued to her.

"We got a deal," the older one said in his thick accent. "But one hundred dollars too much. We give you half. Consider it experience because you are so young."

Will glanced down to the gun. It shined in the sunlight. "That weapon isn't even available for purchase yet. You're not just paying for the weapon, gentlemen. You're paying for the expense it took to bring it over here. And I don't need to remind you; you already made the purchase. The negotiating is over."

The men began speaking to each other in Russian. Will knew he was in trouble now. This deal had been a mistake. Usually, he only dealt with those that someone in his life had vouched for. But times were lean for everyone, even arms dealers. And he'd taken this appointment based on the word of a man he didn't know named Mark Low. Mark was a street thug and general low-life, but he was connected to a world Will had never been invited to. The type of world where people fix the World Series and intimidate members of Congress.

"No," the older one said, "one hundred too much. We pay fifty." The man took out fifty dollars in cash and threw it on the bed as his lackey began wrapping up the gun in the thick blankets Will had carried in with him.

Will swallowed. This was the part of any deal he hated the most. "I'm afraid, gentlemen, that I can't let you take that gun."

The two men looked at each other. The younger one grinned, and then just continued wrapping up the gun.

"Gentlemen, I made myself clear."

"And what you do about it?" the older one said. The

Russian brushed aside his suit coat, revealing the black handle of a pistol underneath.

Will grinned. "Well, in that case, nothing. Fifty dollars would be fine."

The older one turned with a smile for only a moment as the younger one was saying something. Will, his heart pounding in his ears, rushed him.

He hit the older one with a haymaker that caught the poor bastard square on the jaw and sent him sprawling on the bed. The younger one reached for a pistol.

Will tackled him around the waist. He had a gun, too. He'd be a fool not to bring one. But the last thing he needed was a murder beef, even if it was self-defense. Who would believe him?

The Russian brought up his knee, bashing it into Will's groin. Knocking the wind and just about everything else out of him. Will slammed his fist into the man's face. His knuckles felt like they broke and he knew he couldn't do that again. Instead, he tried to pin the man. To smother him with his chest. But the Russian was bigger.

He flipped Will over onto his back. Now it was his turn to slam his fist down. The Russian cocked back and swung. Will moved his head at the last moment, and the Russian impacted against the floor. He yelped in pain as the crack of his knuckles echoed in the small room.

Will seized the opportunity and, from his back, swung with a left and a right, and kept swinging. Until his hands were so bloody, he couldn't see his knuckles anymore. The Russian was going out, blood pouring out of his nose and mouth. He tipped over to the side, and Will let him fall. Will cocked back again, ready to deliver a final blow, but the man was down. And he'd be damned if he'd be the type of person to hit a man when they were down.

Slowly, he rose to his feet, out of breath. His suit coat was wrinkled and his tie was askew. He fixed his tie as he turned to the older Russian who was still laying flat on his back on the bed. Will heard a noise and leaned in close. The man was snoring.

While the older one was still unconscious, Will searched through his pockets. He found the wad of cash. There was at least five hundred dollars there. He took out fifty, and the fifty that was on the bed, and stuffed them into his pockets. He replaced the remaining cash in the man's suit.

"Thank you for your purchase. Please come back soon," he mumbled as he walked to the door.

The weather in Los Angeles couldn't be beat. As Will strode down the sidewalk, tipping his hat forward as two women passed in front of him, he thought back to the weather in New York, and it sent shivers down his spine. Winters so damn cold your fingers would fall off if you didn't get your gloves on in time. And summers so hot it felt like you could melt right there into the pavement.

But Los Angeles didn't have either extreme. It was nice and sunny, not too hot and not too cool, all the time.

He could've taken a taxi but chose to walk instead. The weather was so pleasant he forgot his hands were covered in blood. A pharmacy was just up the road a bit, and Will ducked inside. He ran to the bathroom in the back, turned on the faucet, and stuck his aching hands underneath the cold water. The water in the sink turned a light pink from the blood and swirled around as it drained.

He stared at the water a long time until it turned crystal clear. It reminded him of the trek across the country to California when water was the most difficult thing to find, and the most valuable. The trek that killed his father. His mother had already passed, and the only living relative Will had was his daddy. When he was gone, he was by himself.

His father died of black lung and, toward the end, was spewing frothy pink blood from his mouth that Will would clean diligently.

He sighed and looked up into the mirror. Moving aside a strand of hair, he adjusted his suit and left the bathroom. The clerk behind the counter eyed him but didn't say anything. Will gave him a wide smile as he headed outside.

A good two miles up the road, far enough that he could see the Hollywoodland sign up in the hills, he turned inside a five-story office building. He jogged up the stairs to the second floor. A wooden door with frosted glass was there, prominently displaying the name, "Curtis & Co." The "Co." standing for Cal Diamond. Who refused to have his name as part of the company name, on the stationary, or even registered as one of the owners.

Officially, Curtis & Co. was an insurance agency and even had a handful of clients. But unofficially, a certain segment in the city knew what their actual business was: selling weapons. Pure and simple.

Some arms dealers tried to fool themselves into believing they were doing something noble. They would say things like, "I'm providing for the defense of the defenseless," or "I'm patriotic." It was all nonsense, Will knew. You weren't a real arms dealer until you sold weapons to the enemy of your countrymen—no patriotic sentiment about it. And as far as defense, who the hell knew what people did with the guns once they were sold? It could've been defense, but it could've easily been something else.

Will nodded to his secretary; a buxom woman named Becky, and worked his way through to Cal's corner office. Cal had his feet up on the desk and was reading the paper. Will sat across from him and threw the $100 in cash on the desktop.

"What happened to your hands?" Cal said.

"Mark's buddies weren't as straightforward as he made them out to be."

"They tried to rip you off?"

Will nodded, glancing down to his knuckles, which swelled like grapes. "The deal got done, though." He exhaled and leaned his head back. "Is this what we're gonna be doin' when we're fifty, Cal? Getting into fights with thieves?"

"You tell me a better way to make a hundred thousand dollars a year, and I'm all ears, bucko."

"I just got a bad feeling about all this in my gut."

He went back to his paper. "Wellsir, life's unpredictable. You just gotta roll with the punches. Besides, we're rich enough you don't have to go out yourself. We can hire someone for that."

"I like selling to people. If you don't like what you do, you may as well find something else."

He shrugged. "Tyler Walden called for you."

"About what?" Will said, pulling a package of cigarettes off Cal's desk and lighting one.

"I don't know. Something to do with a British ship and delivering a package."

2

Most of the day was spent at the office, pretending to work. He did have an insurance client call with questions about their life insurance policy, and Will answered like a real insurance agent. He'd studied up to make sure he knew what he was talking about.

After the client hung up, he looked out the window and realized evening was falling. He had a party to get to. He rose and grabbed his suit coat off the back of his chair and headed out. Cal wasn't in anymore, but Becky was, and she said, "Have a good one, Mr. Curtis."

"Becky, you got kids, right?"

"Yes, sir. Two."

Fifty of the hundred dollars he had earned today was his. Cut in cash and hid from the tax man. Will had it in a money clip in his pocket. He took it out and placed it on the desk. "Buy your kids something nice."

He walked out, leaving Becky speechless. Considering she only made $40 in a month, that was quite a little bonus.

The party was at the Millennium Biltmore. Will took

a taxi down, and the driver was sipping at a flask. "You want some?" he said.

"I'm fine. Thank you."

The Biltmore was one of the finest hotels in all of Los Angeles. The lobby was something that could've come from a king's court, or so Will thought. Imported rugs covered every inch of floor and paintings of scenes from the Renaissance were up on the walls. The ceilings were all skylights and frescoes—a place for presidents and industrialists to stay when they came to the city.

Someone in Will's position, a lowly arms dealer, should've felt ill at ease in a place like this. But he always could mix with whatever crowd he happened to find himself in; whether that was on skid row, or in the most expensive hotel this side of the Mississippi.

The party was a cocktail party thrown by a socialite, a woman named Victoria Burden. Victoria was old fashioned in the worst sense of the phrase. She came from a time where the rich were rich and the poor were poor, and it was nearly impossible for that to change. Upstarts, which is the word she and her brood used for men like Will Curtis that rose from poverty to wealth, were typically unwelcomed in her world. Except for that pesky little fact that money bought power, and Will, at least within this city, had power.

He wasn't wealthy enough to buy politicians outright. But he and Cal could certainly rent them from time to time.

Will made a habit at these things to find Victoria first before anyone else and say hello. She invited him, because not to invite him would have been considered an insult, but Will knew she hoped he wouldn't show up. So, even though he didn't really enjoy himself at these things and much preferred a working man's pub, he came every time and every time said hello first.

"Victoria, so good to see you." As he leaned in and kissed one cheek and then the other, he could see her cringe. "You look lovely as ever."

"So glad you could make it, Mr. Curtis. Why with your busy schedule and all," she said mockingly. Everyone knew what Will really did for a living and how little time it took him every day.

Will grinned. "For you, my dear, I Will always make time. Now where is that wonderful husband of yours?" Just like everyone knew Will's profession, everyone knew Victoria's husband was having a fling with his assistant and was probably there right now.

"He'll be here shortly," she said with venom in his voice.

"I'm certain he will. If he's not too exhausted, please send the chap over to me for a drink. Delightful as always," he said, bending down and kissing the back of her hand.

As he walked away, he couldn't help but smile.

The cocktail party was attended by both the new rich and the old rich of Los Angeles. Though the old rich weren't really that old. But they were certainly increasing their wealth while the rest of the country was suffering. Will had seen the shantytowns himself while traveling across the country with his father. Cities made of tin and whatever scraps of wood the inhabitants could find. They would tie them together and hope they held up enough to provide a little shade during the summer and a little warmth during the winter.

Roosevelt's work projects tried to alleviate the pain of starvation. But the jobs were limited, and the ones in power granting them gave them to those that they favored. Will knew some of them took a piece of the salary for themselves, too. He had no doubt the boys in Washington knew about it, if not outright taking a piece too.

And, for some reason, as the rest of the country suffered, the rich grew richer. Maybe because labor was so cheap, maybe because the government didn't have the money to enforce the laws like they once did. Whatever it was, the rich were thriving, including Will. There was no shortage of people looking to buy guns and figure out new and inventive ways to kill each other.

Will scanned the party for somebody he actually wanted to speak with and didn't see anyone. He'd had his fun with Victoria, but boredom at these things settled in quick. It was time to leave. As he turned to head out, he saw a little bird at the bar wearing a tight black dress. Her red hair, not orange like most but actual blood-red, came down in curls over her flawless back. He walked over and stood next to her.

"A Seven and Seven, please," Will said to the barkeep.

The woman glanced at him but said nothing. Will saw the ring on her finger. Not a wedding ring. Something akin to a tribal ring. Encrusted with jewels and appearing decades old.

"Kenyan, right?" he said.

"Excuse me?"

"Your ring. It's Kenyan."

"Oh, I don't know," she said bashfully. "I got it as a gift."

"May I?" She held out her hand. He took it gently in his and ran his fingertip over the ring. "It's a roho ring."

"What's that?"

"A spirit ring. See, some of the tribes in Kenya, the

Bantu for example, they think when someone dies, you can take their spirit and place it inside one of these rings. For safekeeping. And then when you wear the ring, they give you advice and wisdom to help you in life."

She raised her eyebrows. "Wow. You know a lot about rings."

"Well, I travel a lot. But there is something I don't know much about that you can help me with."

She grinned. "And what's that?"

"See, I don't know what I'm going to be doing tonight."

"Oh, that is a problem."

"Indeed it is. So perhaps you can help me with this particular conundrum?"

Will's drink came. The woman took it from the bar top and drank it down herself before placing the empty glass in front of him. "Play your cards right, and maybe I can suggest someone to spend the evening with."

Will opened his mouth to answer, but before he could, he felt a hand on his shoulder. He looked back to see Tyler Walden standing there appearing surprised.

"Will, I called you."

"Little busy now, Tyler. We can talk later."

"I think we need to talk now. As in right now."

Will sighed and turned back to the woman. "I am sorry, my dear, but apparently something can't wait. Will you be here when I return?"

She reached out and adjusted his tie. "We'll see."

Will was forcibly pulled away, Tyler tugging at his arm like a child trying to get the attention of their parent.

Tyler had always been a unique friend to Will. He wasn't particularly bright in most areas, but he had a few select areas that he excelled in more than anyone Will knew. When it came to history and politics, no one knew more than Tyler. When it came to social graces, no one knew less.

"So," Will said, ambling around on the hotel's expensive Persian rugs, "what's so important that you pulled me away from a goddess like that?"

"This is big, Will. Huge," he said excitedly. "Bigger than big."

"All right," Will said, smiling, "calm down and tell me what it is."

"This is retirement money. Enough for both of us. And Cal."

Will stopped, thinking if he looked his friend in the eyes, it might calm him down some. "Tyler, what is it?"

"So you know the British were caught off guard in this war, Will. Churchill ranted for a decade that it was immoral to disarm, but no one listened to him. They thought they made peace with Hitler. That they'd never come to this point."

"Yeah, and?"

"And they're desperate. The German's are a smooth war machine. They had time to prepare. The British were caught with their pants down. So they're desperate for weapons. I mean, Roosevelt is sending aid to them, of course, but nowhere near what they need. So the British have reached out to other channels."

"What other channels?"

"Us, Will. They're using arms dealers to funnel weapons into the war."

Will removed a cigarette from a gold case in his pocket. He lit one with a match and inhaled before answering. "What kind of weapons?"

"Not rifles, although I bet they wouldn't say no to those. What they want is heavy machinery. Tanks, artillery, planes—"

"Planes?"

"Yeah, planes."

"Tyler, where in the hell would we get a plane from?"

"Doesn't matter. This is a once in a lifetime opportunity. We make the deal first and then we work out the particulars later."

He took another puff, lowering the cigarette afterward toward the floor. The smoke irritated his eyes. "I've only found tanks once, and that was because the krauts were desperate to sell."

Tyler looked like he was about to jump onto the ceiling and bounce right back. The excitement was flowing out of him. "That's the best part! My uncle James has an old army buddy in Germany right now. In a factory. He's the half-owner or something. They're under government contract with the Nazis, all the factories are. And he said they're not keeping track of what they order. They'll order fifty Panzers and won't count how many they receive. James says they're good at war but not good at administration."

"So where do we come in?"

"We come in because my uncle will have his buddy sell us weapons below cost. He doesn't care because the government's paying for them anyway. So he'll make fifty for Hitler and give us ten at half the cost. And we sell them to the British to use against the Germans," he said, grabbing Will by the lapels. "Is that not the most beautiful thing you've ever heard!"

Will took another puff of the cigarette and watched Tyler. "My daddy always told me if it sounds too good to be true, it is."

"Normally, that's right. But we're in a war. And a war nobody wants to fight but the Germans! Now is the perfect time to get rich."

Will thought a moment, letting the smoke whirl around him. His eyes itched and began to water, and he found an ashtray nearby and put his cigarette out. "I don't know, Tyler. This sounds like nutty biz."

"I know it's bonkers but what do we have to lose? James's buddy is on a plane over here. You have to meet them with me."

"You're as much a dealer as I am, what do you need me for?"

"Don't take me for a ride, Will. You know you're better at this than me. And you have deeper pockets and deeper connections. You've got senators eating at your swanky house."

Will looked back to the dame at the bar. She glanced over her shoulder and smiled. "Fine, I'll meet with James and his buddy. But... not tonight."

3

When the sunlight came through the windows and lit up the room like a fire, Will was still asleep. But it warmed his face, and he stirred and felt the body next to him. The red hair flowed over his pillows and onto his arm. He touched it lightly and ran his hand down her back. She inhaled but didn't say anything.

Will rose and walked out onto his balcony. He lived in Beverly Hills in a house overlooking Wilshire. A few cars were rumbling by and he watched them a moment. Though he was young, he was still old enough to remember the days when his dad had to hand-crank the Model T and get it going. Now, they ran on their own power with little human interaction. He wondered if one day machines would make people obsolete. They seemed better in a lot of ways. They didn't purposely deceive, and they didn't harm or betray.

After a quick drink of coffee, he showered and changed into a gray suit with a white tie. The woman was still in his bedroom. They'd drank damn near two bottles of rum. He decided to let her sleep rather than rouse her.

Besides, maybe she would be here when he got back?

His car was ready out front. Though Will had a groundskeeper, he didn't have a butler or a driver as many with his kind of money did. He didn't like the idea of other people serving him. He could do for himself. So he hopped into his car and got out onto the road.

The wind whipped his hair and he stuck his head out the window. It was fresh and crisp, with a hint of sea salt from the ocean. Now that he lived near the ocean, he could never imagine living away from it.

The Beverly Hills Hotel wasn't far. White with red Spanish tile roof and palm trees around every corner, it was meant to look like paradise. And considering that girls could be rented for the evening from the madams that contracted with the hotel, and food and hooch could be brought in from anywhere in the city, it was pretty damn close to paradise.

He parked in front and the valet took the car. The young man said, "Good morning, Mr. Curtis."

"How are ya, Reggie?"

"Good, sir."

"How's your mother?"

"She's fine. She wanted me to thank you for the job the other day. I made over ten dollars in tips."

"I'm glad to hear it."

Will had hosted a benefit, which he wasn't actually at, that was for the perseveration of some or other historical landmarks. Really, the money raised went to the soup kitchens across the state that were the only source of food for many people. But if he had come out and said that, no one would've donated. There was a real sense among the elite here that you didn't help those in need because they were already receiving so much from the government.

A small café with a veranda was off the lobby and Will walked over, his eyes on the magnificent floor to ceiling windows. They were spotless and he wondered how many times a day someone came out to clean them.

Seated at a table on the veranda were Tyler, his uncle James, and a man Will had never met before. He smiled and held out his hand. James shook.

"How are ya, Jim?" Will said.

"Grand. I just need a little sheba and this trip could be a success."

"Well, we'll see if we can rustle you up some girls." Will turned to the other man and held out his hand. "Will Curtis."

"Dirk Kalb. How do you do?"

Will sat in the empty chair and almost instantly, a waitress appeared. He ordered an orange juice with ginger ale, something his father used to give him as a kid, and then leaned back in the seat and lit a cigarette.

"So Tyler tells me we may be able to do some biz together, James?"

James nodded. "He told you the details?"

"He did." Will let out a puff of smoke. "But what I'm wondering is, what happens if we get caught? I can't imagine the Nazis are going to be too pleased."

Dirk spoke up. "The Nazis are a passing fad. They will lose this war."

"How do you know?"

"Because there are things they care about more than winning."

"Like what?"

Dirk shifted in his seat and looked away. "Things I've heard rumors about, but haven't seen."

Will glanced at Tyler. "Okay. Well, how does it work then?"

James said, "Dirk is the one that handles the shipping manifests. And he's the one that handles the intake forms for orders. So, say the Nazis order a hundred Astra ninety-threes. The factory will produce a hundred of them. But twenty will be shipped to us. Then Dirk will print a new intake stating they ordered eighty and a new shipping manifest saying eighty went out. These will be the official records kept in the factory. But the government pays upfront. They will have paid for a hundred."

"Won't they catch that?"

James shook his head as he took a bite of an omelet that was in front of him. "No. Dirk has been experimenting with small items, and they haven't caught it. He thinks the person placing the order and the person receiving the order on their side aren't communicating with each other. There's no one checking what they get."

Will placed his cigarette down on an ashtray and took a sip of his drink. "Where do I fit in all this?"

"You and Tyler will sell what we give you to the British. There is some flexibility in what we can get, but we will have to supply you a list, and you will have to sell what's on that list."

"And what's our take?" Will said.

"Fifty-fifty. Fifty percent to me and Dirk, fifty percent to you and Tyler. We don't want anyone feeling they are getting a raw deal."

Will ran the figures. He could get a couple hundred for a good rifle, like a Gewehr, but the real money would be tanks and artillery. A decent Panzer cost about thirty thousand to make. If they sold to the British at the discounted rate of twenty thousand a tank and provided them with fifty tanks, they were looking to clear a million dollars just on that one deal.

Enough for Will to retire, as Tyler had said.

"I'm in," Will said.

James glanced at Tyler. "You sure you don't want to hear about the shipping and production schedules?"

Will shook his head. "We'll work all that out later. I'm in. Tyler, get me a list of buyers and the contacts we have with the British government. Let's get moving on this as quickly as possible before this damn war's over."

Once Will sat down with the list that James had provided, he was in awe. The profits they were looking at were enormous. The reality was that the factory wasn't losing any money in all this. The only people getting a raw deal were the Nazis, who Will hated anyway. He'd seen a speech by Hitler on the television and thought the fella looked nuts. But the crowd seemed mesmerized, and he knew trouble was coming.

The phone rang and he rose and answered it.

"Hello?"

"Will, it's Tyler. They want to meet now."

"Who?"

"The British you dope. They want to meet right now."

"I'm not done running the numbers."

"Who gives a flip about the numbers? They want to meet right now."

Will placed the phone down, ran back to his desk, and grabbed a pen before picking it up again. "Where are they?"

"Harry's Bar."

"Really? They want to meet there?"

"What is this, Twenty Questions? We're talking gravy here. Just get down there with the list."

"On my way."

Will grabbed the list and ran out of the room. He debated taking his gun and then thought it would be wise considering he didn't know who he was dealing with. They could be British, or they could not. He got a holster and placed it on with his pistol before leaving the house.

Harry's Bar was a dive. It would've been the type of place Will would enjoy, except that someone was always getting shot or stabbed there. The barkeep and owner had a reputation of turning the other cheek to the goings-on within the bar, and fights were frequently allowed to finish in a back room, which inevitably led to more violence.

Will parked nearby and hurried inside. The bar stunk of urine and moldy wood. He stood at the front, scanning the place, and noticed no fewer than half a dozen men staring at him. A suit may not have been the best option to wear here.

At the far end of the bar in a dark corner, he saw Tyler. He was sitting with three other men. Will walked to him, ignoring the stares of the men who would no doubt slit his throat if they knew for a certainty he had money and was not a copper.

"Gentlemen," Will said, pulling out a chair and sitting down.

Tyler, in his usual high-pitched voice like a child going to a circus, said, "Will, may I introduce Gilmore Hanks and his associates."

"Mr. Hanks," Will said, holding out his hand. Hanks shook it.

"Your reputation precedes you, sir," Hanks said.

"Then let's hope my reputation ordered me a beer." He glanced back and only then realized there were no waitresses.

"Timothy," Hanks said, without taking his eyes off Will, "go get Mr. Curtis a beer, please."

One of the men rose and walked to the bar. It appeared as an act of courtesy, but Will knew that wasn't what it was. It was an act of power. Hanks wanted him to know he was the one in charge. That he had people under him and that he was somehow more important. It was played subtly. Most men might've just boasted about it. Will thought to himself that he would have to be on guard with Hanks.

"So Mr. Walden has informed me that you indeed have a list of possible purchases," Hanks said casually, as though they were talking about produce.

"Indeed I do. Though I must admit, I received this list only hours ago and was surprised by the speed in which this meeting was set. I don't believe I'll be ready to talk price until tomorrow." Will thought he played it well. He had to seem aloof, like he didn't give a damn whether this deal went through or not.

"I don't think that will be necessary. May I see the list?"

Will hesitated only a second, and then pulled it out of his pocket and slid it across the table. Hanks read it for a long while. His subordinate had brought Will's beer, and Will was about to take a sip when he noticed something crusted on the glass. Maybe food, but maybe something else. He decided it best not to have any.

"We'll take it," Hanks finally said.

"Take what?"

"All of it," he said, sliding the list back to him.

Will glanced at Tyler. He wasn't used to being caught off guard in a negotiation. He had planned on back and forth, tit for tat, and long drawn out conversations about the merits of the weapons and the direction of the war. "There's at least three million dollars worth of merchandise there."

"Three-point two to be exact, but I'm assuming a bulk discount of, shall we say twenty percent?"

"Fifteen," Will hurriedly said. Twenty percent was fine, but he couldn't let Hanks dictate all the terms.

Hanks smiled. "Fifteen is agreeable." He looked at Timothy who removed a satchel that was slung across his shoulder. Hanks placed the satchel on the table. "There you will find a hundred and fifty thousand in U.S. currency. Considering that the weaponry will cost you nothing, if that's all you receive it will still be a tidy profit. But you will receive the remaining once the goods are delivered. We have a ship ready that will be leaving on the Eleventh of March, so we require everything posthaste."

Will looked to Tyler who looked down. The British weren't supposed to know that Will and Tyler were receiving the supplies without cost. It lessened their bargaining position. Tyler never could keep a secret. Some men just felt more powerful if they were able to tell people things they didn't know before.

"So you're asking me to trust you with three million dollars worth of our equipment?" Will said.

"I represent the Crown, Mr. Curtis. The Crown does not welch, as you Americans like to say, on a bargain. You will have your money. The goods will be transported on the SS *Britannia* from Liverpool to Freetown, Durban and then Bombay where they will be unloaded."

"If I may, Mr. Hanks, some of these items are outdated. Why would you purchase all of them?"

"Whatever we cannot use will be allotted to our allies." A slight smirk twisted his lips. "We take care of our allies, Mr. Curtis."

Will grinned. "A dig on my country and I haven't even finished my beer yet."

"The fact is, the States should have been involved in this war the moment we were attacked. Such barbarity as the National Socialists cannot be tolerated anywhere in the world, much less between two allies."

Will shrugged. "The boys on the hill see it as a European war, not a world war. If that's true, there's no reason for us to get involved."

"There's every reason, Mr. Curtis. This is not just some war fought over a dispute on borders. We are fighting evil. When fighting evil, one must choose sides. As the States will eventually have to learn."

Will leaned back in his seat. The truth was, he thought the United States should have entered the war already. The ruin of Poland was an atrocity, and he thought the United States would declare war right then and there. But the declaration never came. "I must say, Mr. Hanks, I'm still leery of simply giving you so much equipment without assurances."

"What type of assurances would you like?"

"Perhaps the rest of the money held in escrow at a U.S. bank."

"Very well, if it makes you feel more at ease. But you and I both know the money could be withdrawn at the last moment should we wish. I have contacts here you could not believe. Not all Americans agree that their government should stay out of, as you called it, the European war." He looked to a man that had stumbled into the bar, already drunk, before he staggered up to the barkeep and ordered a beer. "How about you travel with the equipment?"

"Come again?" Will asked.

"Ride on the *Britannia* and ensure that the equipment is unloaded safely. We will have your money in U.S. dollars waiting for you in Bombay."

"I don't think riding on a warship is for me."

Hanks glanced at the other two men. "Well, it's not exactly a warship. It's a passenger liner."

"But why would you... oh," he said with a chuckle. "You have an agreement with the Germans not to fire on passenger vessels, and you're smuggling weapons on them."

"The Germans are doing the same to us, I assure you. But you will be quite safe."

Will thought a moment. He looked to Tyler who nodded. "All right, that's a square enough deal."

Hanks lifted his glass of beer. "To new partnerships then, and a safe voyage for the *Britannia*."

4

Elizabeth Davenport laughed heartily at the man's jokes. He was some captain or some such with the Royal Navy. He dressed immaculately, and even his mustache appeared greased just the right amount to have a small bit of shine to it. He wore the tuxedo like a man that had been born in one and, even sitting down for hours on end, his back was straight without the slightest bit of slouch to it.

"Why Ms. Davenport, I dare say you make a man forget his senses."

She smiled. Poor little fool, she thought. "Surely it is by no machinations, Captain."

"Surely."

The dining hall was filled with the type of people Elizabeth loathed. Those that took and took without giving an ounce back. And they thought the bounty was endless. That they could step on the downtrodden all their lives without a peep from them. But Elizabeth had seen what was coming. Had seen that, though the bourgeoisie was numerous, the downtrodden were legion. The party didn't last long for the oblivious.

"Why, Captain, I'm afraid I must simply retire for the

night."

"Already?" he said, his face twisting into a good imitation of a puppy. "The night has just begun."

"I'm afraid so. I truly appreciate the meal, however. But I simply must lie down. I feel the pangs of a dreadful headache."

There it was, she thought. Let it sit. Let him come to the conclusion, to the question she wanted asked. They were in her hotel, her room right upstairs. It was a small jump in lascivious thought.

"Well... if you could use the company, my dear..."

"Why, Captain, I do believe you are being absolutely naughty."

He smiled. "I am indeed."

"My room is 304. Whether you come or not, the door shall be unlocked." She rose. "Good evening, my Captain," she said seductively.

As she walked out of the hotel's dining hall, she caught a glimpse of the captain in a mirror up on the wall. He was staring at her as a child stares at a toy they're not certain they could have. Good. Let it cook, she thought.

Her suite, the largest at the hotel, was immaculate, and as she opened the door and stepped inside, she was struck with the scent of chrysanthemums. A bouquet was in nearly every corner. A pleasant scent, she had found, was a powerful aphrodisiac.

She slipped out of her evening gown and into a blue nightie she had crafted in India for the sole purpose of arousing the sexual desire in men. Her legs, firm and muscular, were exposed from the thigh down. Her breasts were held up high and appeared perky, and her arms and shoulders were exposed.

Elizabeth sat at her makeup bar and removed the red

lipstick she was wearing and applied a light pink. She then tousled her hair, giving it a more natural, flowing appearance. Then, it was time for the main course.

In a bag she kept under the bed, she pulled out a small bottle of white pills. She strolled to the bar and poured two glasses of white wine. Removing a bowl from underneath the bar, she crushed one of the pills with the handle of a knife, leaving a fine white powder at the bottom of the bowl. She then dusted the powder into the wine—one pill, and one pill only. Even the most stalwart of men could easily die from too much of the brew. But with one pill, a man of Captain Jones's constitution would sleep soundly for the night. Soundly enough for Elizabeth to take his billfold, his keys, and rummage through his flat before daybreak. Then, she would be on the next ship out of Liverpool.

She lit a few candles and lay on the bed. A book was on the nightstand, *Jane Eyre*, and she read for a short time before the door opened, and Captain Jones stood there. His hat was in his hand and he watched her pleadingly, as though asking permission to enter. She smiled at him and lay the book down on the nightstand.

Rising, she stood stiff, her hands behind her back, accentuated her breasts, letting him drink it in a moment before she retrieved the glasses of wine from the bar. She handed him his and shut the door. "I was hoping you'd come."

"Ms. Davenport, I..."

"There's no need to talk," she whispered, dangerously close to him, her lips near his. She dipped a finger in his wine and traced it over his lips. His tongue came out and licked at it. "Let's just drink for now," she said.

They sipped their wine as she turned to the balcony

and opened the doors. A table and two chairs were set up. Liverpool was dark before them, jagged black abominations jutting out of the ground, speckled with lights. She sat at the table and crossed her legs, knowing the nightie ran up to the top of her thigh.

"Ms. Davenport," he said, "people will see."

"Let them see. Come join me."

He hesitated a moment and then walked over. Sitting quietly, he sipped his wine. She grew restless. British gentlemen were so careful, always wanting to display the proper etiquette. She had once drunk with a cowboy from the state of New Mexico and he guzzled his whiskey like water. They were having a lot of fun until he fell unconscious. Elizabeth almost felt bad robbing him… almost, but not quite.

"A toast," she said, holding up her glass, "to possibilities."

"Indeed."

They drank and the captain took a long drink. He placed his glass down and looked out over the city. "You know," he said, "although I'm here on duty now, I was born here."

"Really?" she said, running her fingers along the edge of her wine glass. "It must've changed quite a bit."

"Unrecognizable. It's amazing that just in your lifetime you can see the world change. See places and people you thought would always be there vanish like the wind."

It was subtle and lasted only a moment, but Elizabeth saw his eyelids nearly close. He was fighting and didn't even know it.

"I'm sorry," he said. "I don't seem to feel quite well."

"Nothing a little more wine can't solve." She leaned

forward, ensuring he had a good view of her breasts, and said, "Let's finish our wine and retire for the night."

He nodded. "Yes, that sounds... pleasant." He drank down half the glass and placed it on the table. The Captain rose and held out his hand. She took it, and he led her into the bedroom. They were scarcely to the bed when he turned to her and wrapped his arms around her. As he leaned in for a kiss, she saw the whites of his eyes as they rolled back into his head and he slumped forward. She let him fall with a thud on the carpet, and he started snoring.

"Poor Captain, can't handle your wine," she said, taking out his billfold and keys and throwing them on the bed.

Within five minutes, she was packed and leaving the hotel room; Captain Jones nicely tucked away in the bed. Tomorrow he would wake with a dreadful headache and a good dose of shame, but little else.

Elizabeth didn't bother checking out of the hotel. They had neither her real name nor an accurate description of the person who had rented the room. Outside, the valet ambled around with his hands behind his back—an older man with a white mustache. Elizabeth removed the slip of paper from her purse and handed it to him.

"Return right quickly, ma'am."

The night air was cool but not cold. She looked up to the stars and watched them as the valet brought her car around. She tipped him decently, but not well and not poorly. Valets tended to remember good or bad tips well.

The drive through the city was easy as few people were out. She knew where Captain Jones lived in the quarter. She had known before she had even met him. Research had been conducted for two weeks prior to their "chance" meeting at the cinema, followed by several dinners and shows. Had things moved too quickly, he would have been suspicious. Too slowly and he would grow bored. Elizabeth knew, through years of practice, how to hit exactly the right chord with men. Not too fast and not too slow. Moderation in all things.

The Captain's home was the entire top floor of a tenement building. She parked out front and didn't care now if people saw her; she would be gone in two days.

She strolled into the tenement building and found the elevators. As she waited, she glanced around the lobby. No security was here, as she had seen previously. The elevator dinged and she stepped on.

She rose to the top floor and stepped off into a hallway. Several doors were there, all leading into Captain Jones's suite no doubt. She walked to the first one and tried the different keys until she found one that fit. The door clicked open, and she stepped inside and shut the door behind her.

The suite was luxurious, decorated with imported items from all reaches of the globe. A tiger rug, probably from India, bearskin from the Americas, a lion's head, likely from Kenya, mounted above the fireplace. She smiled to herself as she crossed the front room and peered out the windows onto the streets of Liverpool. A light fog was rolling in and she watched it a good while until she became aware of the most peculiar sensation. As though she were being watched. Elizabeth turned around just as a woman was walking out of a room.

The two women stared at each other. At first, no one said anything. Elizabeth's mind raced. She had been so careful. No one else was supposed to be here.

"I'm so sorry," Elizabeth said with her best smile, "I'm looking for the Anderson's flat. I must be in the wrong place."

The woman, her face stern, took a step forward. "You're one of his whores, aren't you?"

"Pardon?"

"One of his whores. He has many of them you know. You're not the first. So is he meeting you later? He sent you on ahead like his slave, did he?"

"Ma'am, I'm afraid this has been a terrible misunderstanding. I think I'll just go."

"You're not going anywhere. I'm calling the Bobbies."

"For what reason?"

"You've broken into my home. Or did the great Captain Reginald Jones not tell you that this flat, as well as every other he calls home, is my father's?"

"Excuse me, I must be going." She made a move for the door and the woman stood in front of it.

"I told you, you're not going anywhere."

A moment of silence passed between them. Elizabeth's mind had come into focus during the last minute they'd been speaking. This was clearly Captain Jones's wife, and she was hurt and sick of his mistresses. What could Elizabeth possibly say that would allow her to let Elizabeth leave?

"He didn't tell me he was married," she said.

"Would it have mattered?" the wife said.

"Of course it would have. What type of woman do you take me for?"

"The type that comes to a married man's home to wait for him with his ill wife still here."

Elizabeth wasn't certain what to say. The woman had strength to her, and stubbornness. She wasn't going to let her past until the police were called. But that was something Elizabeth could not allow. Not with the Captain unconscious in her hotel room.

"I didn't break into your home. He gave me a key."

"Did he? Well that's new. You must be quite a special whore to him."

Elizabeth felt the anger swell in her. "Madam, I have been quite polite with you, considering your husband duped me into coming here and believing him to be an eligible bachelor. But should you call me a whore again, I will knock your teeth out."

The wife, suddenly, bowed her head low. Tears flowed down her cheeks, and her hands came up to her face. She sobbed as she moved over to the couch and sat down. She was fully weeping now, and Elizabeth had her chance to leave, but something tugged inside her as she watched the woman. She saw her own mother, sitting on their couch when she was a child—crying because her father had gotten drunk and struck her again.

"He can't really be as bad as that," Elizabeth said.

The woman wiped the tears away but didn't raise her eyes. "If I had any integrity, I would leave. But I have none left. I'm old and sick. And I cling to what's familiar."

Elizabeth looked to the door and then back to the woman. She sighed and sat down. "I've known a lot of men in my life, and the one rule I can say for certain is that you do not have to tolerate a bad one. One of the benefits of being of the female gender is that our supply is far shorter than our demand."

The woman shook her head. "I'm dying."

When she said the words, Elizabeth looked down at the woman's hand and noticed the rag. It was a white linen cloth, stained with phlegm and blood. "How long do you..."

"Not long," she said softly. "A year, perhaps. Maybe a

bit more. You are young right now with all of life ahead of you. But you will find in those final moments that the man you love, as flawed as he is, means everything to you. He is your connection to life. And you've robbed me of that connection, just like the others. I curse you, whore. I curse you and all his whores and hope you die a painful death."

The words were like venom, spit out of the woman's mouth with brimstone and fire. Though Elizabeth rarely let the words of others affect her, these cut her deeply and filled her with nagging anxiety that she couldn't quite place. An icy feeling running down her spine: fear.

She rose silently and backed out of the flat, the woman's eyes, still slick with tears, glued to her. Elizabeth backed out and shut the door. Only then did she realize she hadn't been breathing. Letting out a large breath, she felt the trickle of fear in her stomach now.

I curse you whore.

Elizabeth walked to the elevator and tried to push the woman and this entire affair out of her mind. The fact that she had the Captain's billfold still made this a profitable venture, and with the two other men that had been rendered victims in the past two months, this made Liverpool a success. But now it was time to move on. She had a ship to catch to her next destination of Durban.

5

Will sat on his balcony overlooking the city at night. The lights sparkled like gems and he could occasionally hear a car horn from down below. Tyler sat next to him, sucking on a Cuban cigar Will had imported the previous month. Two tumblers of whiskey were on the table between them, and behind them, in the home, were the bags they had packed for the trip. They would be leaving tomorrow for England.

"He was right you know," Tyler said.

"Who was right?" Will said, leaning his head back and blowing out a puff of smoke.

"Hanks. The United States should've joined this war."

"Maybe. But so far I ain't really heard good reasons to."

"This isn't Paraguay, Will. We're talking about France and Britain. Our closest allies. How can we let them fight the krauts by themselves while we sit back and say we're neutral? We're not neutral. Not against this."

"Against what exactly?"

"Evil, Will. If the rumors I've heard are true..."

"What rumors? Hanks said that too. What rumors has everybody heard that I seem to have missed?"

"Dirk told my uncle about it. He says there are camps that the Nazis take people to as prisoners. That they have large ovens there and barrels of ash comes out of the plumes."

Will looked to him. "You're telling me people are saying that the Nazis are putting their prisoners in ovens?"

"Not their prisoners. Civilians. Jews. All the Jews in their territories."

"That's ridiculous. Why would they do that? They have no motive. Can you imagine the resources it would take to do something like that? They'd have to pull those resources from the war. That'd be just plain stupid, and I see the Nazis as plenty of things, but stupid ain't one of them."

Tyler shrugged and took another puff of the cigar. "I'm just telling you what Dirk said. He said he saw one with his own eyes. The people looked like skeletons. Mothers had to watch while their children were taken into the ovens. They get gassed or shot and then put in there. I'm not saying it doesn't sound crazy, Will. I'm just saying, if it's true, we're dealing with evil like we haven't seen before."

Will was silent a moment. He'd seen evil before. Knew what it looked like real close. When he and his father were traveling across the country, there were roving bands of men looking for the helpless. If anyone had anything they could steal or use, they'd jump them in a second and take it. Some of them had guns; some of them didn't. They made do with bats, chains or knives. Things they could find lying about in the towns that had been devastated during the Depression.

One day, he and his father came upon five of these thieving bandits that had gotten ahold of a couple walking between towns. They made the husband watch while they raped the wife. In itself an evil act, but not one that was uncommon. What made the incident stand out to Will was that after they were through, they slit the woman's throat and let the husband live. There was no rhyme or reason for it. They'd already gotten everything they could get from the couple. But they killed her anyway—evil for the sake of evil.

So, although it didn't make logical sense to do it, Will didn't completely doubt that the Nazis would do something like that. You could never overestimate men's capacity for wickedness.

"They're Godless, Will. That's why they can do things like that. They don't believe we're all the children of the same creator. That He's waiting for us on the other side. So to them, human beings are just raw materials."

Will took a sip of the whiskey. "Damn it if you aren't the most depressing person to be around sometimes, Tyler."

Tyler chuckled. The city was in sparkling motion before them as Will put his feet up on the table and leaned back to look at the sky.

6

Will had been to England once before. On a business trip that involved selling numerous rifles to a man that claimed to be a representative of the French government. Will suspected he was actually a thug with a gang that needed guns. But the transaction was still completed. Though Will didn't get to spend much time in England, he was impressed by its sheer age. Back in Los Angeles, the oldest building they had was but thirty years old. Seeing structures that were hundreds of years old filled him with a sense of history that he was, at the end of it all, just one small man on a continuum that would go on forever after his death.

The sky was overcast as they got to the docks. The taxi sped there the entire drive. The streets of Liverpool were narrow, just barely enough to have two cars side by side. But the driver took every turn as though it weren't possible for another car to be on the road.

Will paid him a little extra for actually getting them here alive and then stood before the S.S. *Britannia.*

The *Britannia* was massive. Will knew it would be

large, but he had never seen a ship like it. The ship measured at between 400 and 500 feet, he guessed. Two masts were up, one bow and one stern, and a light gun was on the back, even though it was supposed to just be a passenger vessel.

Workers were busy loading the ship up as Will watched them. He stepped close to the water and leaned against a railing that was there. Tyler was next to him, counting their bags to make certain they had everything.

"I'll tell ya," Will said, "what man can create using nothing but his mind never ceases to amaze me."

"Well, can you be amazed carrying a few of our bags onboard?"

Climbing up the ramp onto the ship, Will glanced back to land. He'd been on ships before, though they were small ones and never for a journey this long. But this was, as Tyler had said, retirement money. And he wanted to see it through himself.

Civilians had begun boarding, but there were plenty of royal navy men there as well. Will and Tyler stood among them, not exactly certain where they were supposed to go. Finally, Tyler stopped one of the crew and said, "We're looking for a lieutenant named Kyle Bixby."

The man pointed them in the right direction, to a command bridge near the middle of the deck, and they trudged over there with their bags. Two men were standing out front discussing something on a chart when one of them looked up. The man was as big as an ox with a gray beard and steely eyes. He had the burst capillaries in his nose of a man who enjoyed his drink and, even from several feet away, Will could smell the alcohol coming from his breath.

"Excuse me," Tyler said with a wide smile, "I'm Tyler

Walden and this is Mr. Will Curtis. I believe we're supposed to be meeting either with you or the captain."

Bixby looked them over and then excused the other man with a nod of his head. When the man was out of earshot, he said, "You're the Americans I'll be babysitting I take it? Your cargo was placed on board this morning."

"I'd like to see it," Will said.

The man stared at him a moment in silence. "What's the matter? Don't trust me?"

"Trust is earned, Lieutenant. Over time and through actions."

"Or through fear," he said with a grin. "Follow me."

They marched over the ship and to a set of stairs leading below. Will had seen some American built ships and the doorways were narrow to conserve space. But the *Britannia* had wider doors and stairs, and corridors that seemed to be meant for walking side-by-side. As they passed the rooms, Will looked in. They were basic, much like hotel rooms, but they also passed an elaborate dining room and a gaming room with blackWill tables and roulette wheels.

Another set of stairs and another corridor with rooms, though smaller than the ones on the higher deck. They were climbing down into the bowels of the ship, one step at a time. A tight claustrophobic feeling squeezed Will the lower they went. Light became a series of bulbs with darkness in between. Until they arrived at a large metal door that needed to be unlocked. Bixby opened it and held it wide for Will.

Inside were hulking masses of shadows. The lights were all off and everything was covered with white tarps. Will walked to the first one and lifted the tarp. Underneath was an artillery gun. He covered it back up. No tanks were in this shipment, but he could just imagine it now. A hundred tanks, all sold by them to fight the Nazis. If this worked, and Hanks actually came through and made other purchases, Will would never have to be concerned with money for his long as he lived.

"Everything in order?" Bixby said.

"Lieutenant, I do believe everything is just fine," Will said, taking out a fresh cigarette and lighting it.

The launch of the ship was done with little fanfare. Will and Tyler stood at the railing, watching a small crowd of people waving as the *Britannia* took to sea. The sky was overcast and the sea appeared foggy and gray. The ocean, though they were still close to shore, was already bouncing the ship around and Will could see a sour face on Tyler.

"You okay?" Will asked.

"Dandy."

Though Tyler disappeared below deck, probably to vomit and lie down, Will watched the shore until it was out of sight. It took a long time. But the rumbling of the engines beneath his feet and the grinding noises from the ship had a somewhat calming effect on him. That man could create something like this to sail the oceans, to think it up and execute it. To conquer nature.

He had always been a worshipper of men. That man could recreate the universe to suit their needs using nothing but their reasoning faculty. That's why a man's work was so important. He attempted to recreate his little section of the world how he wished. Though, he wasn't entirely certain how arms dealing recreated the world how he wanted. Maybe that's why he was here? A few deals and he could be out. Move into a more legitimate business like oil or electricity. Something that would make all those blue-blood sons a bitches in Beverly Hills stand up and take notice rather than looking down their noses at him.

What he ultimately wanted, more than anything else, was a family. People to love and be loved by. He hadn't married yet because this was no life to bring children into, but if he were legitimate, then that would be a possibility.

The fog was light and rolled over the water like cotton balls. Will watched them a while before deciding to take a stroll around the deck.

7

The German ship Thor was what was known as a "Raider." They were combat ships disguised as merchant ships. Captain Stephen Hertz had always liked the term. It reminded him of Vikings from the Norse tales his mother had told him as a child. Growing up in Frankfurt, such tales were told to most children. Though now, under the Reich, they'd taken on special importance.

As he shot down the glass of beer as though it were water, he glanced around the bar. The space was filled with his crew, here for some relaxation before they returned to their patrols.

Patrols. Is that what they called it now?

Hertz had fought in the first war. He was a seasoned naval officer and had understood why war needed to occur. It was like a game of dominos. Drop one domino in the correct place, and all of them would tumble. He didn't agree with the old war, but he understood why it had to be fought. A man was assassinated that shouldn't have been assassinated. Such insults could not be left unpunished.

But this new war, the one they called the Second World War, though it was just the first with a long break in between, this war he didn't understand. The motherland gave concessions and had received concessions in turn; they had grown influential, they had what they needed, and the world was weary of war. But he had seen the men in power and understood them. For men such as the führer, war was the end in itself. Not a means. And he had seen the results of enough men like the führer to know that it could only end with the destruction of one side or another. And the aggressors typically lost. The soldiers on the other side fought for their freedom. The Germans, his men, were fighting for pride. And pride only got you so far.

"Captain," someone said, slapping his back. "You seem sullen. Was ist falsch?"

His first mate, Felix, stood with a grin on his face just a little too close to Hertz. When Felix drank, he always leaned too close, and Hertz had realized that he didn't do it on purpose. Rather than pushing him away, he tolerated Felix until the conversation was over.

"Nichts," Hertz said, shaking his head. "I'm fine. Just tired is all."

"Well, victory is near my Captain. You should be celebrating with the men. Soon, we'll be back in the bosoms of our women with a new Germany before us."

He nodded, staring at the bubbles left in his mug of beer. "Yes, it will be a new Germany, that much is certain."

Behind him, Hertz heard something. Several men shouted, "Sieg Heil." Hertz glanced behind him. Two SS officers had walked into the bar and were greeted with cheers, as though they were conquering heroes. Hertz turned away from them and back to his mug. He motioned with his chin to the bartender, indicating he wanted more. The bartender poured him another, the white foam overflowing from the mug.

Hertz drank down half the beer. Felix had gone to say hello to the SS men. The fawning that took place with them made Hertz sick. He knew what they were. What they really were. And soldiers they were not.

"Herr Hertz," a man said behind him.

The SS officer was tall and lean with a protruding nose, his face freshly shaved. He reminded Hertz of a bird that walked on two legs. He even had the elongated neck with the bobbling head that seemed like it could throw him off balance.

"Guten abend, Commander," Hertz said, returning his eyes to the beer.

"I did not see you at dinner this evening. Did you not receive your invitation?"

"No, I received it. I was busy I'm afraid."

"Busy? With what?"

He drank down some of the beer. "Fighting this damn war."

The commander received his drink of weinschorle, a mixture of wine and mineral water, and took a small sip. He placed the glass down and leaned forward on the bar, his eyes fixated on Hertz. "You know, if I did not know you as I do, and know how loyal you are to the Motherland and our führer, I would almost suspect that you didn't agree with this war."

"A man would have to be crazy to disagree with the führer, now wouldn't he? And I am certainly not crazy."

He smiled, revealing large white teeth. "No, that is not a term I would use to describe you." He took another drink and replaced the glass on the bar. "They say the war will be won in six months' time. That we will establish the Reich across all of Europe and then the world. Do you agree with that?"

"I do not," he said calmly.

"Really? That is surprising. Now, why would you say that?"

He stood upright and looked the commander in the eyes. He knew what was happening. The commander was goading him into saying something against the führer or the Reich. Then he would be arrested for treason. Hertz knew that overcoming adversity was not the true test of a man. The true test of a man was what he did and how he treated others when he had a little power. And so far, he had seen nothing but pettiness and cruelty in the men he once called brothers.

"Just something I believe. Wars always take longer and cost more money than anyone thinks they will."

The commander took another sip of his drink, so small that it hardly lowered the level of liquid in the glass. Technically, Hertz was this man's commanding officer. But practically, that was not how it worked. The SS and Gestapo ran the country. They were the führer's right hand. The military was a tool that he used but cared little about.

"That's true enough," the Commander said. "But why specifically do you believe the war will take longer? You must have a reason."

Hertz inhaled deeply and let it out through his nose before he guzzled the rest of his beer. He laid a few marks on the bar and turned to leave. "It will take longer, because we don't know what we're fighting for, and our opponents do. Excuse me, Commander. I have a patrol to start early in the morning."

Hertz quickly left the bar and the shouting and clinking of mugs behind him. He stepped outside into the cold air and heard footsteps behind him as Felix rushed to his side.

"Leaving already?" Felix asked.

"Don't feel much like drinking right now, Felix. You have fun. I'll see you in the morning."

"I heard what you said to the commander," Felix blurted. "That this war will take longer. We've won almost every battle, Captain. That is insanity to think that."

Hertz stopped and turned around. He looked Felix in the eyes and placed a hand on his shoulder. "I have seen this before. I've seen what men like those that run our beloved country do. They have hubris. They won't win this war. They can't because all they see is themselves and the practicalities will be lost." Hertz stared his first officer in the eyes. "We are going to lose this war, Felix. And heaven help us when we do. Because the world is not kind to the compatriots of evil."

With that, he turned and strode off into the night, his eyes westward on the Atlantic as the waves rolled onto the beach.

8

By the time Will was dressed and slicking his hair in a mirror that hung on the wall of their suite, Tyler was vomiting in a bucket. The man had been vomiting so long, he had nothing left in his stomach, and only bile and saliva was coming up.

"You sure you don't want to come?" Will asked. "Might help you to walk around a little bit."

Tyler shook his head. "I'm not leaving this suite, my friend. First impressions are important and I won't have my first impression with the women of this ship be vomiting over their shoes."

Will adjusted his tie. "I'll pick up some crackers for you. Seasickness usually fades in a few days."

"Fantastic," he said, retching again, the veins in his neck standing out like small snakes.

Will left the suite and made a note to bring back some soda water, crackers and whatever else they had on this ship to deal with that.

He made a quick stop above deck and walked toward the bow. They were in the open sea now, drifting in the

Atlantic like flotsam lost in a world of water. The stars were like nothing he'd ever seen before. A thin, milky film seemed to connect them, like a blanket that was thrown loosely over them. And they were so bright that, together, they nearly outshone the moon, which was only a crescent slit tonight.

Will had been out of the country many times. He traveled a lot since he wanted to be the personal salesman for Curtis & Co. But maybe Cal was right? Maybe you became the boss specifically so you wouldn't have to do the actual work anymore?

But even thinking it filled him with nagging anxiety. He enjoyed people, all people, and the finest part of this gig was that he met people from all over the globe. Met them, and then convinced them to buy what he was selling. If he had to just sit in an office all day like Cal, running numbers and dealing with lawyers, bureaucrats, and accountants, well he'd just as soon find something else to do.

After a few more minutes walking the deck, letting the night breeze softly touch his skin, he went down below deck. The corridors were filled with people, and he smiled and nodded to as many as he could. He was in a jovial mood, as starting an exciting journey was prone to put him in, and he felt like being friendly to everyone.

It seemed that almost everyone headed one way and he followed the herd until he arrived at the casino he'd seen before. Only this time, you could hardly see the gambling tables. Men and women—dressed well, but not lavishly—crammed into every space. Throwing away their hard-earned cash on a moment's distraction and the slim opportunity that the casino on the ship, perhaps, didn't understand the art of taking their money as well as an established joint on land.

In Will's experience, the casinos at sea knew this. And they hired the best and the brightest dealers and pit bosses from land to oversee the operations. Losing money was not something any company tolerated.

As he rounded a blackjack table and came to a craps table, he stopped. He wasn't sure if he meant to or not, but he did. Stopped right there in his tracks and someone from behind bumped into him. The bump snapped him back to where he was and he said, "Excuse me," though he didn't move his gaze.

The woman blew on the dice for luck. She tossed them over the table. They bounced and rolled to a hard ten and the people surrounding the table cheered. She was beautiful in a way that required no makeup, no elegant jewelry or dress—one of those natural beauties that nature had chosen to stand above everyone else.

She was playing with other people's money. A man, dressed in a finely tailored suit, stood next to her and would throw cash on the table with each roll. Then he would kiss the dice, then her hand. She allowed it before blowing on the dice and tossing them.

As she leaned over the table to get a good throw, Will watched her other hand. It dipped into the stickman's stash of chips and she would slip a few into her palm. After the throw, everyone would either cheer or clap in encouragement, not even noticing her hand dropping the chips into her purse.

Will knew instantly that the woman was as dangerous as a cobra. But there was nothing in the world he wanted to do more than go over and introduce himself. He slipped past the people watching the game to get beside her.

Growing up in the Depression, the two skills Will developed above all others, were the ability to read people and tell them what they wanted to hear, and the ability to steal without being detected. Developing and practicing those skills was not a matter of choice. He was either good at talking and stealing, or he and his family would starve. His father, an alcoholic seemingly since birth, couldn't provide for the family when the Depression hit. That task fell on Will's shoulders. And at ten years old, his opportunities for employment were limited.

As the woman tossed the dice, Will slipped one hand into her purse and collected the chips she had thrown in there. He palmed them and slowly put them in his pocket. Within three rolls, he had her entire take. And then he slid away and watched.

The woman rolled again, winning, and the crowd around her cheered. She whispered something like, "I've had enough for now," to the man that had been putting down the money and turned to leave. The man grabbed her and told her to stay, and she, with a million-dollar smile, slipped out of his hand and said, "Maybe later."

The man watched her walk away. Will knew she'd probably cash her chips on another day. She wasn't greedy or in a hurry. She could wait. When she was palming the chips, she could've quickly taken the one hundred dollar chips, but she didn't. She took the one and two dollar chips. Something that wasn't easily noticed by the boxman, dealers or stickman at the table. Four employees of the casino were just ripped off right under their noses, and they each had a smile on their face while she did it.

Will followed her as she strolled around the casino.

Men would glare at her, and some would make comments. She would smile, say something that would make the men smile back, and then casually slip away. Every man she did that to couldn't take his eyes off of her. She was an expert in seduction. Looking at it objectively, she'd already seduced him, and she didn't even know he existed.

After making the rounds at the casino, she left. Will followed her. She went up to the deck into the night air. As she walked to the railing, overlooking the sea, she glanced around and then stuck her hand in her purse.

The moment was priceless. The look on her face was as though she'd just discovered that some aspect of reality she always thought true was a lie. The woman scrabbled in her purse, at one point even dumping the contents out on the deck and going through them. Will grinned as he walked to her.

"You okay, Miss?"

"Fine. Thank you," she said, startled. She began picking up her things and putting them back in the purse.

"Are you sure? You look like you've lost something."

"I'm fine," she said sternly.

Will took out the chips and shook them in his hand. "Then I guess you won't be needing these."

Slowly, she rose to her feet. Their eyes locked in the light of the moon. A few floodlights were on the ship, but they didn't reach here. She'd chosen the darkest part of the deck. Will wondered if she was instinctively that good or if it was just an accident.

"What do you want?" she said.

"You can have your chips, and my silence to the casino, in exchange for one thing."

She straightened. "And what's that?"

"You have dinner with me tonight."

The woman, who up until now had a face of stone, softened. She grinned and reached into his hand and removed the chips, placing them back into her purse. "Deal. But you pay."

9

Once Hertz stepped aboard the Thor, he knew he was in his element. The sea had called to him as a child and it was land that he now felt uncomfortable on. And it was something he'd seen in nearly every seaman he'd ever met. They would lament the sea and the months or even years away from home they would spend upon it, but they would always return.

Hertz had studied the myth of the Sirens, the lovely creatures in Greek mythology that would woo passing sailors onto the jagged rocks with their beauty and sweet voices. He believed the Sirens were an allegory for the sea itself.

As he stood on the deck and watched the sunrise, he wondered if today would be the day he died. Every day, he asked himself that question, and so far he'd been extremely lucky. And that's all it was. They could give him as many medals as they wanted for surviving battles and wars, but he knew it wasn't skill that led to his survival. It was just pure, dumb, unexplainable, luck.

"Captain," Felix said as he hurried to him, his hands tucked firmly into his coat pockets, "we're ready."

He nodded. "Then let's not make a big spectacle of it."

Felix stood by a bit longer, staring at the deck as the ship rocked lightly with the waves. He stepped over to where Hertz stood and leaned against the railing. "I've been thinking all night about what you said. That we will lose this war."

"And?"

"I think you're right. I think I've known it for a long time. I'm scared, Captain. I'm scared for my family back in Berlin. The world will not forgive us twice."

With that, the two men stood silently and watched the sea. Hertz couldn't think of what to say. He saw what was coming as clearly as though he were watching a motion picture. There'd been rumors that the Reich intended to betray their alliance with Stalin. That, Hertz knew, would be the turning point for the war. Russia was a cold, desolate place with people hardened by centuries of conflict and starvation. They would not stop until one of them was utterly destroyed.

Hertz saw the fear in his officer's eyes. He slapped his shoulder and said, "You're a good soldier, Felix. Get our ship moving. Work helps us clear our minds and makes our soul crisp."

"Yes, Captain."

As Felix returned to the bridge, Hertz looked out over the sea. It wasn't violent, but the waves were churning in long, open rolls and lifting the ship and then dropping it like a toy in a child's bath.

He sighed and then left the railing to head for the bridge.

10

Will sat across from her in the dining room. There were two dining rooms on the ship, one for use by everyone, and one for use by "VIPs." Though Will wasn't sure what exactly made a VIP. He was not on any list so it took some cash to convince the maître'd otherwise. Luckily, Tyler had gone to an exchange when they'd arrived in the UK, and they had British pounds rather than U.S. dollars, which the man insisted he would not take.

They were sat against the wall at a small table. The linen was exquisite, as was the décor, but the space was small. Meant for a crew to eat buffet style, not for passengers to dine at their leisure.

"So," she said, leaning back.

"So," Will said with a grin.

"You certainly don't seem to have any qualms about blackmail, do you, Mr..."

"Curtis. Everyone calls me Will. And you are?"

"Elizabeth."

"Elizabeth. That was... my mother's name actually."

She giggled. "I'm certain if I had said Heidi that would

have been your mother's name."

"No, it was Elizabeth. Everyone called her Bethy, though."

"And where is your mother that just happens to be my namesake?"

Will pulled out a lighter and a fresh cigarette but didn't light it. He flicked the lighter and stared at the flame. "She passed away."

"I'm sorry."

He nodded. "What're you doing on this ship, Elizabeth? Other than stealing from poor infatuated craps dealers?"

"Odd, I was going to ask you the same thing. Someone with your skill certainly isn't here for the convenience of travel by ship."

"I like traveling by ship. I like the ocean. The vastness of it."

She nodded. "Because it makes you feel so small."

"No, the opposite actually. That it's so vast and so powerful, and yet we've managed to conquer it with our minds. To sail across it to anywhere we want."

"Conquer it? I dare say you haven't been at sea enough if you think we have conquered it."

"We're sailing on top of it halfway around the world. What would you call it?"

"I'd call it an invasion of the natural world. And not one that the natural world takes kindly to."

Will smiled. "You're a pessimist."

"No, I'm a realist."

"Who wants to live in reality when there's so many places more fun?" The waiter came, and they ordered a bottle of wine and an appetizer of oysters. "Where did you learn to do that?" Will asked.

She shrugged as she took a sip of wine. "Simple sleight of hand. I was living with a magician for a while. That's the career path I thought my life would take."

"What changed?"

"Life. The magician was arrested for stealing from the audience and I was left destitute, so I had to use the only natural weapon I had. My wits."

"You have more weapons than that."

"If you're going to be crass, I think our dinner might be over."

"No, not that, I meant your beauty. That's what distracted the dealers. They were so busy staring at you they didn't notice your hand in their chips."

"Well, I hope that's not all there is. Beauty fades and I would hate to think what happens to me if that's all I've been relying on." She drank down some more wine and placed the glass on the table. "And what about you? What do you rely on to survive?"

"I survive because I can read people. I know what they want. And I've made quite a fortune giving it to them."

"And what do they want?"

Will was about to light the cigarette when the oysters arrived. Despite his aversion to anything even resembling seafood, they looked delectable. He poured some lemon juice on it and the oyster meat was delicious. The fluid left in the shell tasted of the ocean. Salty and thick on the tongue. He had two before he lit his cigarette and leaned back in the seat, watching Elizabeth sip at her wine. "To answer your question, they want what they can't have. Simple."

"That's it? They want what they can't have?"

He nodded. "And as soon as they can have it, they no

longer want it. So the trick is to give them just enough that they always want more. That they always think they don't have enough."

"And what is it you give them exactly?"

He shook his head, taking a puff of the cigarette. "Honestly, it doesn't really matter. Right now, I give them weapons. But I could just as easily give them whiskey or trousers. The principle is the same. They need to feel wanted and loved. I give that to them."

She grinned and leaned forward, placing her elbows on the table. Will noticed her hands. They were delicate with nails as pure and clear as water. "You're a romantic."

He chuckled. "Maybe."

Elizabeth finished the wine and motioned to the waiter for another. "Mr. Will Curtis, I do believe you and I could get along just dandy."

He blew out a puff of smoke and watched her, the way her eyes sparkled in the lights. "I was just thinking the same thing."

11

Over the coming days, Will couldn't think of a single thing he wanted to do more than see Elizabeth. After their meal that first night, they'd walked the deck in the darkness and talked for well over two hours. Will felt connected to her instantly. They shared a common background, one in which they both had to rise above circumstances to survive. But more than that, they seemed to share a philosophy that they were more than the sum of their parts. That they were special somehow, carved out for a unique destiny.

Though Will enjoyed every second he spent with her, he was worried that she was with him solely to kill time. Other than dining and the casino, there wasn't exactly a lot to do on the ship. It was possible she was only spending time with him because she was bored.

Today, they were supposed to play blackjack at the casino and then have drinks in Will's suite. He was amazed, after visiting her cabin, how lovely his suite really was. Hanks had certainly sprung some extra dough for them to have pleasant sleeping quarters.

As Will ran up to the deck, he saw a vision before him of feminine beauty in a way he'd never seen it before. She dressed in a white dress that came to just above her ankles. A sunhat was on her head, and her lips were painted a dark red from lipstick that contrasted with her milk-white skin.

"All dressed up and nowhere to go," she said by way of greeting.

"That's not completely true. We can gamble."

"I'm sick of gambling. We've been gambling for almost two weeks."

Two weeks, Will thought. Has it been that long?

All he remembered were days spent reading and eating, and nights spent getting drunk with Tyler and Elizabeth. After a while, he didn't even count the days anymore. In fact, he wasn't exactly sure what day it was now.

"Have we been on this thing two weeks?"

"We have."

She reached out and held his hand. It sent a small spark of electricity through him. Though they hadn't made love, they had kissed once. Out on the deck by the light of the moon. Will had wanted to take it further, but Elizabeth was patient and subtly let him know that she was not interested in sex with him yet. Insecurity again reared its head, and he wondered if she wasn't interested because she wasn't interested in him, or because she was as fascinated with him as he was with her and she wished to savor it. To enjoy every touch, every glance and kiss.

"We'll be to port soon. I think Durban's the next stop. You ever been to South Africa?" Will asked.

"No. I've never actually left Europe."

"Really?" he said, staring at the way her fingers dangled casually over the railing. "You'll love it. It's a mix of Arab and African. A lot of history there. Wars between Moslems and Christians left a lot of scars and decimated buildings."

"Can't wait," she said.

"You look worried."

"Not worried. Just anxious."

"Why?"

"I don't know," she said, looking at him with her sparkling eyes. "Just a feeling in my gut, I guess. We started with an escort of four ships, and now the escort's gone."

"That's standard practice. We're in the middle of the ocean now, not likely to see Germans out here other than merchant ships."

"I know. But just being at sea so long makes you focus on all the little things that could go wrong."

"Well, my dear," he said, taking her other hand, perhaps you could focus on me instead."

She smiled, and let him lead her down below deck.

When Will awoke the next morning, he was alone in his suite. Tyler had met someone, too. Women were somewhat scarce on the *Britannia*, and the woman Tyler had met was not really of his type. He usually preferred the blue-bloods of Los Angeles, the high-end types that drove Will insane. The ones that were all outward appearance and no substance.

But there was no one like that here. So Tyler went on walks and had his meals with whoever would say yes to him. He'd one night brought back two attractive women that were part of the ship's crew. Though Will flirted and drank, his mind never drifted from Elizabeth. He mustn't have been good company because the girls eventually lost interest and left.

Last night, he and Elizabeth had laid in the dark and watched the moonlight come pouring through the windows of the suite and fill the room with a blue glow. They'd grown wholly accustomed to the rocking of the ship by now, the movement of the ocean, and it no longer registered with them. To them, the world seemed to stand still as they lay in bed and listen to the sounds of the waves.

Will fell asleep in her arms. When he awoke, she was gone. He had an urge to check his pocketbook and belongings. It would be just like her to leave with whatever she could carry. But for some reason, he knew she hadn't.

As he went above deck after dressing, he saw that a small crowd had gathered on the port side of the ship. They were watching something in the distance. Will lit a cigarette and with nothing better to do, ambled over. He could see, just barely, what they were observing.

It was another ship.

12

Hertz had heard the ship from deck long before the crew let him know it was there. Hearing was the best of his senses. Occasionally, in the darkness of the sea at night, sound was the only thing a person had.

The other ship was a passenger liner, or what was advertised as a passenger liner. German analysts had picked up wires long ago that stated the British were smuggling weapons on their passenger ships. They even let actual passengers go on board. A dangerous gamble, and one that Hertz thought was unnecessary. It's not like he could see who was or was not on the ship.

Though the proper place of the captain was in the command center, that's not where he wanted to be. If he was going to fire on this ship, he wanted to see it. And not through some tube of glass and mirrors, but from the deck of a ship, as his ancestors had done centuries ago. He would stare at the vessel as he destroyed it.

Felix ran up behind him. "Captain..."

"Bring the ship aft. Get the gun crew ready... Wait. They're moving."

Hertz lifted the binoculars that hung around his neck. He read English and could see the vessel was named the *Britannia* and that it was turning in the sea. "They're running from us, Felix."

"What do you want to do?"

"As soon as we're in range, begin the first salvo."

Will saw the vessel up close now. His own ship had turned in a wide arc. He thought maybe they were on a collision course or that the other ship might not be able to see them; something innocent.

That's not what it was. And he didn't realize it until he saw several of the crew sprinting to the *Britannia*'s guns. They were ramming shells into the weapons like madmen.

The other ship was a dark gray and seemed much faster than the *Britannia*. As he stared at it, Will suddenly felt the jerk of momentum. The engines rumbled underneath his feet like an earthquake, and he knew the ship was speeding up.

Tyler sprinted up from below deck, still throwing on a jacket. He spotted Will and ran over. He appeared flushed, like he'd been vomiting and was rudely interrupted by all this.

"What the hell is going on?" Tyler said.

"I think we're under attack."

"What?" he scoffed. "Not a chance. We're in the middle of the Atlantic Ocean. Nobody's out here."

Will turned back to the gray ship. It was rushing toward them, and Will knew right then this was a lost battle. The vessel was a warship. Not a passenger boat smuggling weapons. The thing had an array of guns on the deck; some long, and some short and thick. He had no doubt it could take them out in a second.

"Tyler," Will said, his eyes never leaving the gray vessel, "I think we better get to the lifeboats."

Before Tyler could respond, Will saw several flashes from the guns on the other ship. They appeared like little explosions, flames bursting out of the weapons like puffs of breath from the mouths of men in the winter air. Nothing happened at first. As though the guns had popped blanks. And then the sounds started.

The high-pitched scream rained down from the sky and drew near, though the shells were undetectable by the human eye. They were traveling much too fast.

A massive burst of water exploded in front of the ship, at least forty feet high. They had missed, but just barely. Will looked at Tyler, and before they could run, another high-pitched scream echoed through the air.

The ship rocked as though it had rammed into a building. Flame and the shrieks of dying men and women filled the air around them. Will felt the heat from the explosion as though he'd fallen in a campfire. It didn't touch him. In fact, it was on the other side of the ship near the stern. But the shell had hit their main gun and sent a burst of heat and flame over the deck.

Much of the crew was made up of Indian engineers and gunners. Most of them on the main gun were gone. Some of their bodies lay on the deck, mangled, burned and in pieces. The screams of the passengers watching the salvo echoed as they ran below deck, the squeal of the shells showering down upon them making Will's ears ache.

Tyler hit the deck. Will grabbed him and lifted him

by his collar. They dashed for the stairs leading below just as another salvo began. And then the *Britannia* began firing, too. Loud booms that deafened him. The shells were traveling faster than the speed of sound and rumbling the entire ship. But they weren't enough. The *Britannia* got off six rounds just as twice as many rained down on them from the sky.

Many of the gray vessel's shells slammed into the ocean near them, throwing up the massive columns of water that looked like erupting volcanoes. But many of them hit. One struck the deck near the center of the ship, raining fire over the crew scrambling to help the passengers get below deck. Another hit port, nearly swinging the *Britannia* to its side. The ship jerked down and forward, sending everyone on deck off their feet.

"Shit!" Tyler screamed.

Will pulled at his arm. He thought to run below deck, but that was useless now. These weren't warning shots; they meant to take the *Britannia* down. The lifeboats were the only way off the ship.

As he pulled Tyler along, the screams of the twisting, heated metal and the sonic booms deafening them, a single thought pushed its way into Will's mind: Elizabeth.

He stopped dead in his tracks. He turned to Tyler. "Get to the lifeboats."

"Where are you going?"

"I have to get someone," Will shouted over the din of another shell slamming somewhere into the ship, rocking it like a seesaw up and down. Tyler grabbed his arm.

"She's not worth it."

Will pulled away. Nothing he could say was going to convince Tyler, so he didn't feel he needed to try.

Will dashed down the stairs, ramming through

crowds of people heading below deck. He knew they hadn't realized the ship was sinking. They thought they were safe because they weren't exposed. Like children covering themselves with a blanket to protect against monsters.

The people crowded around Will like a sea of ants. They swelled to the point that they nearly knocked him off his feet and he had to grab a railing on the stairs to keep his balance.

It would be no use shouting for her. The air was filled with screams, explosions, and the squeals of the shells. Before he could choose a direction to run, the ship lurched to the side. So much so that if he hadn't been holding on to the railing he would have flown into the wall. A great mass of people wasn't so lucky, and they slammed into everything around them. Wall, ceiling, floor, and doors. But once they were down, Will had a clear run to the casino and dining hall, which were near the stairs leading farther below deck and to Elizabeth's cabin.

He made a run for it, leaping over the fallen men and women who were scrambling to their feet. One man jumped up and turned right into him, knocking both men over. Will pulled himself up and leapt past the man, not waiting to check if he was all right.

He ran past the dining hall, which was packed with people cowering from the chaos outside, and then the casino, which was closed and locked. The stairs leading down were two flights, and Will took them as quickly as possible, pushing his way past those that had decided the stairwell was the safest place on the ship.

He leapt to the lower level and sprinted down the corridor, shoving people out of the way. One woman was down on the floor, leaned up against the wall. Blood was cascading down her forehead onto her dress, and her face was bruised. She'd been trampled. Will stopped and knelt.

"You okay?" he shouted.

"I can't find my mother. I can't find her... I was here with her."

Will glanced around. Everyone was so panicked, he was worried she might get trampled again. He pulled her off to the side into a small room. "Wait for me here," he said.

He ran down the hall and burst into Elizabeth's cabin. It was empty. After running back into the hall, he found the woman from before. He took her arm and lifted her as he pushed forward.

People weren't moving. They had decided to stay put, which was good for him because he could easily shove them away and get past them. But some people were going in the opposite direction and it became a shoving match between them. One man, a large fellow, tall and with broad shoulders, knocked Will so hard he hit the wall. But the woman, at least, was unharmed.

The stairs were going to be difficult to climb. They were narrow and packed tightly with crew and passengers. Will had to really shove to get by them, and several tried to hold him back. But he held tight to the woman and pulled her up to the top level and then to the deck.

The air smelled of spent gunpowder and smoke. The ship was on fire in several places, and no one was trying to put it out. Suddenly, Will heard a signal. Some alarm, and he wasn't sure what it was. He'd never heard it before. But some crewmen were near him and they interpreted for him as they shouted, "Abandon ship!"

Everyone made a rush for the lifeboats and Will looked to the woman. But she wasn't a woman, not really. She was just a girl. Perhaps no more than fourteen.

"I don't know where my mother is," she said, panic in her voice.

"Let's get you safe and I'll look for her," Will said. Though how he would do that, he had no idea.

He dashed, the girl in tow, to the lifeboats. And that familiar screaming filled his ears as a detonation of such proportions rocked the ship that many of the lifeboats shattered to pieces of sharp, splintered wood—embedding themselves into the flesh of the passerby.

People were tossing things overboard, hoping to get a few of their items into the lifeboats that had been lowered and were now in the water. Will pulled the girl behind him as he ran to the nearest one. Two crewmen were helping lower the boat into the sea.

"She needs off this boat."

"We're not loading yet," one of the crewmen said.

"She's just a kid."

The crewmen eyed the girl and then Will. He then held out his hand and Will pulled the girl's hand up to the crewman's who pulled her on board the lifeboat. Will watched the boat, or what was really just a large, white canoe complete with oars, lifted and then lowered into the water. There was still space, and the crewmen helped more people into it. A few jumped from the ship and swam over, helped in by others.

Will scanned the deck for Tyler but didn't see him anywhere. Only a handful of lifeboats were left, most of the rest destroyed or set on fire. He wondered if it was chance, or if the other ship had specifically not wanted the passengers to be able to flee.

"Will!"

He turned to see Elizabeth. Running to her, he saw that all order and civility had vanished. Everyone had a sense, if not actual knowledge, that space on the lifeboats was limited. Will grabbed her and ran back to the last two lifeboats left.

13

The *Thor* had been struck twice, but hardly seemed to notice. One of its guns was no longer working, and at least two crewmen were dead, but other than that, the ship was in pristine condition. The *Britannia* had been caught entirely off guard. How was that possible, Hertz thought, when they were in open water attempting to aid in the war effort?

He peered through binoculars at the ship. A large hole at the bow was sucking in the ocean. The ship didn't have long.

Hertz walked to the small set of narrow stairs leading up to the command center and shouted, "Felix!" before turning back to the *Britannia*.

Felix ran up and stood next to his captain. "Jawohl."

"Stop the salvos."

Felix looked to the *Britannia*. "But it's nearly sunk, Captain."

Hertz lowered the binoculars. "I said stop them."

He nodded. "Jawohl."

Felix ran back up to the command center as Hertz

stood on the deck of his raider and felt the hum of the engines beneath him. Despite himself, he had enjoyed that. The crash of the enemy vessel being torn apart by his guns was something that even invaded his dreams. And he didn't know if that made him an animal, or just human like everyone else.

The guns stopped firing. That would give the passengers enough time to get to the lifeboats. Felix trudged back down the stairs. To his credit, he had never once mentioned to Hertz that perhaps the captain should be at the helm. He knew Hertz fought in the open, somehow needed the sun above him and the open sea air against his face. When cramped into a confined space, Hertz felt ill at ease. Claustrophobic. Like he was trapped in his own coffin.

The silence was deafening. Both ships sat on top of the swells as they bobbed the vessels up and down. But the *Britannia's* position was shifted. It was tilted forward, taking on water so quickly that it was beginning to lift the stern into the air.

Hertz ran back to the stairs and the command center on the flying bridge. He took the ladder quickly and came upon several of his men discussing the *Britannia*. They stopped and went quiet when he arrived. The men glanced at each other and Felix was the only one who spoke.

"Captain, I think we should keep firing."

"We will. But give the passengers a chance to get to the lifeboats."

"Ah, prisoners then? I'll prepare the pickup."

An intense revulsion filled Hertz. An image came to his mind, uncalled and unwanted. He had been taken on a tour of a facility that everyone else had heard rumors about. He was a war hero, a decorated captain in the Reich. And the powers that be felt he had a right to know what it was they were doing. What they were fighting for.

He saw men as thin as skeletons with eyes that bulged out of their heads as though they would fall out at any moment. They were covered with lice and dirt and huddled together as they were either worked to death or slated for execution.

He thought about retiring from the military when he saw it, perhaps even feigning injury, but he felt if he stayed, he could be put in positions to fight the orders of his superiors. To do things they wouldn't do and maybe, just maybe, reduce the wickedness his countrymen had introduced into the world.

"We won't be picking up any prisoners," Hertz said.

The men looked at each other. Felix was the only one who could ever speak his mind freely, and he swallowed before he said, "Captain, we have them. We have won. We can bring back hundreds of prisoners if we wish."

"And where would those prisoners end up, Felix? Hm? Do you know? Have you seen where they end up? Answer me."

Felix looked down to the floors. "Ja, I've seen it."

"Then why would any man, any man with even a sliver of humanity left in him, send another human being into the hands of those devils."

"Because they are our orders."

The simplicity of the statement, the directness, touched Hertz. Felix wasn't an evil man. He wasn't one of those that had designed those camps or instituted the policies of slaughter that the world would likely never forget. He was a soldier following orders, not realizing that some orders were not to be followed.

"Felix," Hertz said, calmly placing his hand on the man's shoulder, "there are some orders that you must make a decision over. Are you a man, or are you a machine? If you are a machine that does whatever it is told, then so be it. But if you are a man, a man with a family that has a mother and father that care for him, a man that has experienced life and gained judgment, if you are such a man, then you must realize there are some orders that you would rather die than obey."

Felix, his face contorted in confusion, just nodded. Hertz patted his shoulder.

"Having said that, we have sunk the *Britannia*, as was our duty as soldiers. But we have no duty beyond that. No duty to hurt these men. Warn them that another salvo is about to be fired and give them time to flee... and then sink the *Britannia*."

14

Will knew they'd been assigned lifeboats when they had first arrived on the ship. But he didn't remember what his was. And Elizabeth's, lifeboat six, had been destroyed. Will ran, pulling her behind him, to the edge of the starboard side. A lifeboat was there with about six people inside.

"You need to jump," Will said.

"What about you?"

Will glanced back over the deck. It was littered with dead bodies. The *Britannia* was now at the complete mercy of the other ship, and he wondered why they hadn't been finished off yet.

And he didn't know where Tyler was. Probably on a different lifeboat. So he could either find Tyler, or stay with Elizabeth, but not both. Or, he could stay on the ship and hope that his intuition was wrong and that it wouldn't sink. A mayday had no doubt already gone out, and someone would be by to pick them up. Assuming the Germans, or whoever the hell they were, didn't finish them off.

He looked at Elizabeth, to her eyes and the way they flickered with fear. Fear, but not terror. Even under these circumstances that would break most men, she was steadfast. She was a woman that had been through enough to know that panic served no purpose in survival.

"Okay," he said, "I'll come. Let's go."

The only way into the lifeboat now was to jump. Will helped Elizabeth onto the railing, and then he climbed up. The water was about thirty feet away and coming up toward them in high swells before dipping low again.

"We'll jump when the water's at its highest."

Elizabeth slipped her hand into his and he glanced at her. Even here, under this pressure, with men dying around them, with alarms piercing the air and an enemy vessel drifting around them like a hungry shark, even here, just the act of holding her hand made his heart flutter. And he knew he'd made the right decision. He'd be staying with her, no matter what happened.

"Jump!" he shouted.

They jumped. The air was against his face for only a second until he slammed into the cold water. It sent shivers up and down his body and he'd lost his grip on Elizabeth's hand. Will opened his eyes. The water was murky and he couldn't see more than a few feet in front of him. But he could hear the sounds. Loud splashing as men jumped overboard, the whooshing sound of oars hitting the water and being pulled through. Then, it went quiet.

The *Britannia's* engines had been cut, and an eerie silence descended... just before the groan of metal echoed so loudly that it hurt his ears.

He burst through the surface, slicking his hair away from his eyes, and looked behind him. The groaning, which he thought could easily have been the earth opening up to swallow them, was the *Britannia*. Its stern had lifted out of the water. Not enough to be noticeable, not yet. But the ship was sinking bow first.

Will couldn't see Elizabeth. He swung around in a circle. "Elizabeth!"

A small voice answered him from not far away. "Will!"

He saw her then, her arm sticking out of the water as her body was sucked under by a large swell. He swam toward her, in that loose, head above water stroke that was common among people that had never been taught technique. But he was fast, and he was nearly to her when something hit him and he went under. Someone landed on him from the deck of the ship.

Will hadn't been prepared and didn't suck in a good breath when the next swell hit him. He was pulled deeper into the darkness of the sea. The light above him was now in fragments and seemed a million miles away. He kicked furiously and seemed to make little progress.

Then he saw Tyler's face. Tyler grabbed his arms and both men kicked and clawed as they reached the surface. Will sucked in air like a man lost in a desert who had just been given a goblet of cold water. He saw Tyler struggling and grabbed him and pulled him to his back. He lay back as well, his line of sight to the sky as he kicked toward the lifeboat.

Soon, he felt hands on him, pulling him up and onboard.

The lifeboat had about fifteen people now. Elizabeth pushed through them to get to him. She bent down and said something to him, but he couldn't hear her. He realized then that all he heard was a sharp ringing in his ears and wondered if a shell had struck nearby when he had been underwater.

Tyler was coughing next to him. Wet and exhausted, but alive.

Slowly, the ringing in his ears subsided, and Will could hear the shouts of men.

"That's it!" someone shouted. "Shove off, now!"

A sound unlike any other filled Will's ears. Somewhere between a building collapsing and a plane crashing into asphalt. It was the final assault. The final salvo. And it had struck its target perfectly. The hole in the bow of the *Britannia* was wide and gaping. Pulling in the ocean around it. And the stern was now in the air and slowly, like some goliath waking from sleep, rising.

"Paddle," Tyler shouted as he grabbed an oar and threw one to Will. "That ship's gonna suck down everything near it when it sinks. Paddle!"

Will thrust the oar into the water and paddled as hard as he could. Until his arms burned and his shoulders felt like they would fall out of their sockets. His back hurt, his legs hurt, his neck and hands ached. Everything hurt, and he hadn't even been paddling that long.

He looked back just as the ship groaned again, and the stern rose up like some monster into the air, and the *Britannia* began to be sucked down into the darkness of the sea.

15

The paddling continued for a long time, until they were completely clear of the *Britannia.* And even from there Will felt the resistance in the water. The *Britannia* was, like Tyler had said, pulling everything into its grave with it. Will saw one lifeboat that hadn't gotten far enough out. It reversed course, speeding directly backward. It made him think of a toy in a bath when you pull up the stop and the water drains.

The lifeboat was sucked down and crushed, the people disappearing underneath the waves. Will turned away.

Finally, after what seemed like hours but was likely no more than a few minutes, the rowing stopped. Will placed his oar down and leaned back. No one said anything as the last of the *Britannia* was sucked underneath the waves.

The people on the lifeboat numbered sixteen and about half of that was crew. While the *Britannia* sunk, they stood straight in the lifeboat, tears streaming down a few of their cheeks. When the last visible part of the ship was gone, they sat back down.

The lifeboats were stocked with provisions; Will knew that much, but wasn't sure if they had water. One of the crewmen he recognized as Bixby. The man, before appearing larger than life, now seemed to be small and defeated. It wasn't the best time to approach him with questions, but Will had to know.

"How much food do we have on here?" he asked.

"A week's worth. Give or take a day," Bixby replied without looking at him.

"What about water?"

He shook his head. "Water's too heavy to carry."

Well that's dandy, Will thought. You could survive for a couple of weeks without food. In fact, in the dust-bowl of the Midwest on their trek cross country, he and his father had to go nearly six days without food. The pain in your stomach would come in waves, like it was trying to eat itself, but for the most part it wasn't the worst thing Will had been through. But even a couple days without water was debilitating. He remembered dry, cracked lips with blood that seeped out the last of the body's moisture. Headaches and migraines that would blind you before you felt the pain in your guts, the pain of your organs shutting down.

The people on the lifeboat with them were quiet, each contemplating their own scenarios. Some were probably thinking about how quickly they would be rescued, others about revenge on the bastards that had done this. Will thought neither of those things. His only immediate concern was water.

He rose and said, "I'll be right back," to Elizabeth and Tyler.

As he made his way across the lifeboat, Bixby eyed

him but said nothing.

At the bow of the lifeboat were several plastic chests. Will opened the first one. They were supplies. Food, medicine, flares—anything they could need except for the most important. How had someone designed this without considering how they would get water?

Bixby came up behind him. His face smeared with black soot, and a head wound that was bleeding down his cheek. Will wondered if he looked similar.

"We're gonna need these chests for water," Will said.

"I doubt we'll be out here that long. The SOS went out quick. And it looks like the raider's gone."

"They don't attack the rafts?"

"Normally, I would say they do. But they were probably nervous that we had ships on an intercept course. Bloody krauts turned tail and ran like girls."

Will looked at the sea around him and was acutely aware that no other lifeboats were in sight. At least a dozen had gone into the water, and now they had all drifted in different directions. "So do we row to land?"

Bixby chuckled. "You can row all you want, Yank. Don't think it'll do much good. The sea's taking us where she wants us to go."

Will, suddenly, grew uncomfortable around Bixby. About the way he was staring at him, like Will was an unwelcome visitor in a world he knew little about. Without showing an ounce of anxiety, he kept his eyes locked on the large Brit as he brushed past him and back to the stern of the lifeboat.

He collapsed next to Tyler, suddenly aware of the profound fatigue that penetrated his muscles. And there was a pulling sensation in his hip. Like it was out of place.

"You okay?" he said to Tyler.

He nodded, unable to speak. Tyler turned his eyes to the ocean and lay his head back against the stern. The lifeboat bobbed lightly up and down with the swells. But the sounds were pure ocean. Nothing humanmade whatsoever. No ships, no shouting, no cars, phones or televisions.

And for the first time ever, Will suddenly felt that his life was not in his own hands.

16

The weather alternated between soft sunshine filtered through clouds, and the deep gray of a coming or leaving storm.

The air had a salty taste to it, and no one had spoken for hours. Anticipation was like energy, and he could feel it in the lifeboat. Everyone was holding on to the hope that they would be rescued before nightfall. Though no one had said anything, Will could sense that's what it was. The survivors didn't want to be out here in the dark.

He looked at Elizabeth, who had fallen asleep. Her dress was waterlogged and dirty with soot. Her hair was matted, and half came down to her shoulders and half was still up. But he didn't feel her beauty had been diminished a bit. She had a strength to her that was extraordinarily appealing, something akin to his own resilience at life's surprises. The other men on the lifeboat would glare at her lustfully, and it amused him. Even in this situation, having gone through what they just went through and watching their compatriots die, the pull of their loins was still too powerful to resist.

He saw nothing but lust in their eyes. It was curious to him for a moment until it hit him that they didn't see in her what he saw in her. When they looked at Elizabeth, they saw flesh. He saw something deeper.

"I don't like him," Tyler whispered.

Will looked to where Tyler was staring. He was looking square at Bixby. "Why not?"

"Something about him. He seems... cruel."

"I didn't get that impression."

"That's because you're strong, Will. You don't have to worry about cruel men. For me, I gotta be on the lookout for things like that. And I've developed a sixth sense about it."

Will watched Bixby, Tyler's words ringing in his ears. The defeat he'd seen earlier was fading.

The man was huge. Naturally huge, not the type of size that came with effort. He was tall with shoulders that seemed to go from one end of the lifeboat to the other, and his hands were scarred from a lifetime at sea. His face had that weathered look people got when they spent too much time fighting sun and wind. He was, Will had to admit, an intimidating man.

"I'm sure we'll be picked up soon," Will said. "No need to worry about him."

The day dragged by painfully slow and for the first time, Will got a hunger pang. He was accustomed to such things and it didn't bother him. But what did bother him is that they'd only been out here hours and he was already hungry.

Elizabeth woke from a nap sometime around noon, as the sun was overhead. She smiled when she saw him and then looked down to her sullied dressed and the shoes that were scuffed and torn. "I thought this was a dream," she said grimly.

"No," he replied, "but I'm sure it won't last too much

longer. Bixby says the SOS went out as soon as we were hit. I'm sure they'll be by soon to pick everyone up."

She looked to the others on the lifeboat. "How many survived?"

"I don't know. Maybe half, maybe less."

She shook her head. "All those lives... and for what? The egos of madmen that sit in their capitals."

"We're all madmen, Ms. Davenport. Some of us are just more comfortable with it than others."

Will stretched his legs out before him, his knees aching from the position he was sitting in. "You never did tell me where you were from," he said.

"Does that really matter now?"

"If you'd rather sit in silence that's fine, but I'd rather talk."

"That was rude of me. I'm sorry. I didn't intend for it to come out that way."

"It's all right. People act differently in crises."

"You say that like someone who's been in a lot of crises."

He shrugged. "I don't sell rugs or flowers. So there's a certain danger involved in what I do."

She was silent a moment. "That ship... when it first struck, I was below deck. I thought we were in the middle of a storm or had hit aground. And then there was an explosion that shot fire through the decks. A man was there in front of me and the fire got onto him. It burned him over half his body until someone could throw a blanket on him. And then... you could see right down to the bone."

Will nodded. "War is the worst of men's creations. My daddy said that after fighting the krauts in the first war." He perked up at the thought of food. "But let's leave the grim talk for later. We're on the ocean, it's a beautiful day, and we're in good company. Let's enjoy it before they come to pick us up."

She gave a sad little smile and said, "I wish I had your optimism."

"You do. You just have to believe it."

Her eyes drifted over the water. "I'm not certain I can."

17

The food on the lifeboat had been tallied. Enough for one small meal a day for each passenger for six days. Six days, Bixby assured everyone, was a lifetime after an SOS. Skiffs were probably already out at the wreckage and searching for survivors right that moment. There was nothing to worry about, he said.

Will didn't believe him. He had an edge to his voice, like he was forcing the words out. Something was wrong, and Bixby wasn't revealing what it was.

They ate their first meal around what was probably three or four in the afternoon. Only one man on board had a watch, and it was so soaked with water, it no longer functioned.

The meal consisted of crackers and dehydrated meat that tasted oddly similar to the crackers. They had some MCIs onboard, which Tyler explained to Will were Meal, Combat, Individual rations, but these were in cans and not opened. Bixby, as the highest-ranking officer on the lifeboat, was the one deciding which rations and how much should be spread around to everyone. Will said nothing. The fact was, he was no leader and never had been. Not really. Perhaps if he had any inclination for it, he would have been. But right now he was more than happy to let Bixby fill that role.

As the boat drifted along with the swells, Will noticed the debris in the water. Not only was there the usual debris one would expect when a ship sank, but bodies had come, too. The corpses didn't look real. Like mannequins from some awful nightmare. Torn apart, charred, or bloated and white.

Among this wasteland of bodies, something was moving. A table with someone on it. A man that was smoking a cigarette. The man sat on the upturned table as it drifted with the sea, a cigarette dangling from his mouth. Will could only tell because of the thin trail of smoke.

"Hey," he said, "there's someone out there."

Bixby looked to him and then shaded his eyes with his hand. He squinted, right in the direction of the man and then shook his head. "Too far out."

"What're you talking about? He's right there. Let's pick him up."

"I said no."

Will rose to his feet. "I'm not going to sit here and watch that man drown when we've got plenty of room."

"Aye, we have plenty of room. And how much food do we have, Yank?"

Will hadn't thought that way. Wasn't accustomed to it anymore. That man was another mouth to feed, and the already slim portions of food they had would have to be split even further. But he didn't care. He wasn't going to watch a man drown when he could do something about it.

"Pick him up," Will said coldly.

"Will," Tyler said, "it's all right. This is a life or death situation."

Bixby, his eyes fixated on Will, didn't move. "Listen to your friend. I'm the ranking officer on this vessel. If you don't like that, I'm certain there's some room on that man's table."

Will went to take a step toward him and felt a soft hand on his shoulder. He looked over to see Elizabeth standing next to him. She didn't say a word, just gently applied pressure to his shoulder until he sat back down next to her. Bixby had a smirk on his face.

The man on the table was drifting farther away. Will watched him as long as he could. But after a short while, he disappeared. Will hoped he was still floating, somewhere that would take him to an island and civilization.

When the man was out of sight, he stared at Bixby, who met his gaze.

As his attention faded from the man, the most immediate concern became the ship itself. By the time evening fell, water up to their ankles had filled the boat. The crew of the *Britannia* began baling out the water using anything they could find, one man even using the cap off his head. Will and Tyler joined in. Cupping their hands and throwing the water out a little at a time. But the water was coming in faster than it was leaving. A leak.

Bixby and two of his men were leaning over the side of the lifeboat, scanning from the bow to the stern. When they had found the leak, one of the men jumped into the water after taking off his shirt. He shoved the shirt through the small hole and was then lifted back into the lifeboat.

But they had a bigger problem. As was typical in the

ocean, darkness was falling quickly. The sun was setting and it appeared, from the flat ocean, to be falling right into the water. The sea was lit a bright gold and Will couldn't help but sit and watch.

"Listen up," Bixby shouted, "we need watches set throughout the night. You'll be looking for water inside the boat to bale out and for any lights in the dark. When you see a light, you're to wake me or my first mate Porter. I'll be on the first watch and we'll go right down the line here to the bow. We gots us enough people to take one hour shifts. We ain't got no watches so you'll have to guess how long an hour is."

Will sat back once the sun was nearly gone and stretched out his legs. The sky was dimming so fast, it appeared like someone turning down a light. And as night overtook them, Will felt Elizabeth's head on his shoulder as she slowly fell asleep.

18

That first night, a lot of things went through Will's mind. The shaking of the *Britannia* as she was hit. The rumbling of the engines underneath his feet that felt like small earthquakes. The sirens that were so loud they felt like they could make his ears bleed... And the final, gurgled, wet sound that the siren had become as the ship rose vertically in the air and was sucked into the sea.

He had a dream he was back on the deck and watching the silent fire that blew out of the raider's guns. The shells were falling around him, but he couldn't run. His legs wouldn't respond to him.

After a long time, step by painful step, he was able to get to the railing and lean over, staring into the blackness of the ocean. And deep below the surface, he saw something. A faint glow, like moonlight but coming from the ocean floor instead of the sky.

And as he looked up, the raider fired its final salvo, and the ship lifted out of the sea, throwing him forward with such violence he slammed into the deck and broke every bone in his body. The ocean, the water an inky-black, sucked him down into darkness. Above him, he saw puddles of oil set on fire. And the more he tried to break the surface for air, the more the ocean drank him down.

He woke with a start, the sky a pure black above him. The stars were like gems and the night was silent with the exception of the rolling waves. A man stood over him, his face only visible by the light of a half moon.

"Your turn for watch," the man said.

Will looked around. Elizabeth and Tyler were asleep, as was everyone else. Despite the predicament, the soft rocking of the ship and fresh night air lulled people to sleep. By now, Will's wet clothing had dried, everything except his socks and his shoes. He slipped them off, exposing waterlogged feet and rubbing them with his palms to warm them up as he watched the moon above them. From down here, with literally no other light, you could see the crevices or mountains or whatever the hell was on the moon. He wondered if the moon had rivers and oceans like the earth did. If people once lived and worked, and died there.

He stood up and decided to get some blood into his legs. The lifeboat, though in the shape of a canoe, was large, and he'd heard someone earlier explaining that it was meant to hold fifty people. If that were true, Will thought, why hadn't they prepared food for fifty people? Or water? Someone hadn't done their job. And now he wondered how many people would die because of it.

As he paced the lifeboat, he observed the faces of the men that had survived. Some of them were hardened, he could see it even in the dim moonlight. Faces worn by time and effort. Some of them, probably just passengers that were unlucky enough to board the *Britannia*, looked frightened even in their sleep.

Men.

Will realized Elizabeth was the only woman on the lifeboat. An icy sensation went down his spine as he looked back to her. He had seen what men could do to each other over women. The lengths they were willing to go to court affection. And if that affection wasn't reciprocated, many men turned to beasts. No matter how civil they might have seemed before.

A sound pulled Will away from his thoughts. Splashing. It was coming from near the boat. Slowly, he stepped to a spot on the port side of the lifeboat in between two men. He leaned over and looked into the sea.

A single fin cut across the water. About two feet high and gray, though in the moonlight it appeared ghostly white. The fin was like a knife and split the water in a perfect V behind it as it circled the lifeboat. Slowly, it sank back beneath the surface.

The sharks had already come, though there was no dead around them anymore for them to feast on. Vultures of the sea. But something would have had to draw them here, and he didn't know what would've done that.

Bixby was nearby and he turned, a grin on his face. The big man was lying on his back, a pack tucked firmly underneath his neck. "For every fin you see, there's five you don't."

"Why are they here?"

"They're curious. And there's a trail of dead behind us. They'll clean them up right and then follow us, hoping something on board is edible."

"They can't possibly be smart enough to know this is a ship."

"Most ain't. But there is one that is. The White Death.

Most sharks don't know they're in the water and there's a surface world up here. But the White, he knows. He comes up and looks around, around the surface waters. It knows it's a shark, and that it's in the sea. Which means it knows that this is a ship and that edible things are inside of it."

Will shook his head. "They're not that smart."

"Really? And how many Whites have you come across in your profession of counting money, Yank?"

"My profession isn't counting money. My profession is killing men." It wasn't totally true, but Will felt the infantile response to a bully. To puff out your chest and act as tough as he was.

"Well, killer of men, then you should be quite handy on this voyage, shouldn't you? I got a feelin' we may need some killin' done before this is over."

With that, the big man lay his head back and closed his eyes. Will watched him a moment and then made his way back to the stern, keeping his eyes on his feet so he didn't trip. The last thing in the world he wanted right now was to be in the dark ocean with sharks circling the boat looking for corpses.

He sat on the transom, then changed his mind and sat on the deck. Elizabeth stirred. She opened her eyes and saw him and smiled.

"I would give anything right now for a bottle of wine and a hot bath," she said. "And we've only been afloat one day."

"Well, when we get rescued, I'll buy you whatever bottle of wine you want and you can have the largest, hottest bath we can find."

"I can provide both for myself quite well, thank you very much."

He looked at her and saw that her eyes were still closed. "Why do you do that?"

"Do what?"

"Act as though you don't need anyone else in the world?"

"Because I don't."

"Balls. Everyone needs someone. Even you." He pulled out his package of cigarettes, which had been entirely waterlogged, and his lighter. The lighter would flick a flame, and the cigarettes nearly fell apart in his hand. He was about to toss them overboard when he decided he better hang on to them. Just in case they miraculously dried out somehow later.

"Do you really think we'll be rescued soon?" she asked. Her voice was different now. Different even than this morning when she had spoken to him defiantly. Now her voice was soft, full of apprehension and a youthful optimism that she probably wasn't used to feeling.

"I think so. We aren't the Nazis. People mean something to us."

19

Will stayed up all night after he had been roused. It was Tyler's turn for watch, but he didn't wake him. The restlessness of being stuck somewhere wouldn't let Will go back to sleep. He may as well keep watch.

The ocean had its own sounds through the night. Sounds people weren't meant to hear. Sounds only shared by the animals that lived there. One thing he did hear constantly was splashing as a shark whipped itself, slicing through the water with that crescent tail. Will didn't look at them much, but he couldn't help but listen to them.

In the morning, Bixby gathered everyone together. At least everyone that he wanted. Will rose and joined the group of about four men, the ranking officers that survived the *Britannia*. They gave him an odd stare but didn't ask him to leave.

"African coast's the closest," one man said. "Probably about nine hundred kilometers away."

Bixby shook his large head. "We'd be goin' against the wind. We need to head to Brazil."

"That's almost two thousand kilometers. It would take us weeks to get there."

Bixby shrugged. "It would save us on the oars 'cause the sails would be doin' all the work."

Will interjected, "Why don't we wait for rescue right where we are?"

The men looked at him like he was a fool. Bixby said, "Do you know how wide an area they have to search? They'll never find us."

Will didn't say anything. He wasn't an experienced sailor and, like Elizabeth, had held out hope that rescue would be coming soon. He hadn't realized that the people that knew what they were doing had already given up on the idea.

"Brazil it is then," Bixby said, looking each man in the eye. "Anyone think different?"

No said anything and Bixby began barking out orders. He wanted to lower the mast and hoist the mainsail, neither decision Will understood. But he waited there until the men scurried off to do what he had asked.

"These people need some food," Will said.

Bixby looked around. "I decide when we need food. Once a day is all we can manage. We wait until night."

Will didn't argue with him. What was the point? Bixby was clearly the man in charge, and everyone seemed to defer to him. Besides, he agreed with him. If for nothing else than they would have something to look forward to throughout the day.

Back at the stern, Will spoke to Elizabeth most of the day. He told her about his trek across a devastated United States. About the time he traveled to Guatemala and was bitten by a monkey. He told her everything he could think of, and he didn't know why.

For her part, she listened quietly. He couldn't tell if she was interested or not, but she acted the part well and never tried to interject with her own stories.

Tyler didn't speak. He leaned against the transom and stared off in the distance, looking pale and frightened. Will knew, just from that look, that Tyler was a man whose life had never been threatened before. There'd probably been fevers and accidents and things, but he had never before been put into a situation where the odds of survival were less than the odds of death. And he was shaken.

"You holding up?" Will asked him.

"I'm fine."

"You sure?"

He looked to Will, his face unchanged. No smile or grin, no look of frustration or anger. "I said I'm fine."

By about midday, Will noticed water in the lifeboat again. He rose and scanned the boat. The water was streaming in from the port side, and he leaned over and saw two planks loose. Bixby was busy at the helm and Will walked to him and said, "We got another leak."

As though insulted that Will saw the leak before his men, Bixby gave him a venomous look, but left the helm to someone else and followed him down. The big man looked over the port side and swore under his breath. He shouted, "Thomas! Get yer ass down here."

A slim man with a bald head ran down. Bixby informed him that he would be going over the side of the boat to make the necessary repairs. Apparently, they had some patches of wood and the hope was that they could stuff cloth into holes and then patch them up with some nails that were on board in the utility chests.

The man stripped nude, only once glancing over to

Elizabeth to make sure she wasn't watching, and then was lifted upside down by two other men. His hands held the repair materials, and he was lowered down into the water. He was lowered so far in fact, that at times when the swell rose, his head was completely submerged. But he didn't stop work.

"Got it!" he shouted after a few minutes.

He was hoisted back onto the lifeboat and the leaks had stopped. Out just past the port side, Will saw more fins. The sharks hadn't come when the man was lowered, and he wondered if it was because they were frightened, or because they knew the crew wasn't as weak as they would become later.

The day turned out to be a hot one. Will lay with Elizabeth near the stern all day. He took off his shirt and dipped it into the ocean and would wrap it around his head like a turban. Mercifully, the sun faded quickly and evening fell again. And the time they'd been waiting for had arrived: mealtime.

The rations were distributed evenly. Everyone got the same share—a spoonful of condensed milk, a hard biscuit, and some jerky.

"I swear," Elizabeth said as she took a large bite of the biscuit, "no meal I've ever had tasted as good as this."

Will looked to the sky. Some clouds were gathering farther out and the possibility of rain seemed likely. "Let's just hope we get some water to wash it down with."

As night fell, Elizabeth slept, but Will stared out over the ocean. The sun was exhausting. Will couldn't tell if the deep fatigue he felt was from the heat or the lack of food and water, but it seemed like the sun was what drained him of his energy. He understood why Elizabeth slept most of the time. It was probably the wisest move.

But, though exhausted, he was unable to sleep. Even the possibility of a ship in the distance was enough to keep him awake. And he had seen the flares; they only had three. If someone were to shoot one off unjustifiably, they just reduced their chances of survival by a third.

"I'll tell ya," Will said, "when I get back to LA I'm going to Phil's and getting the biggest damn steak you ever seen. And a glass of red wine with those shallots and potatoes. And cake for dessert. The biggest chocolate cake with icing they have."

Tyler was up but didn't respond. Will looked to his lap and saw the biscuit and jerky untouched.

"Tyler, what's the matter? Are you sick?"

"No."

"Then you need to eat. Who knows how long this food is gonna last. You gotta keep up your strength."

Tyler swallowed before speaking. "Something's wrong, Will."

"Hell yes something's wrong. We're floating on the ocean on a leaky lifeboat."

"No, not that. Something else."

"What?"

"There were sixteen people on the boat when we got on."

"What of it?"

"There were fifteen when we woke up this morning."

Will stared at his friend a moment, the way the moon lit up his eyes a soft white. Tyler appeared like he'd seen a ghost. Pale, wide-eyed and staring off at nothing.

Will looked up. From the stern, he could see down the lifeboat up to the helm. He began counting the men... six on one side, five on the other, one at the helm, and the three of them at the stern. Fifteen.

"Maybe we miscounted before?" Will said.

"The big guy, Bixby, he counted up how many people there were when we first got on. So he could figure out how long the food would last. He said sixteen. I remember it clear as day, Will. He said sixteen."

Will looked out over the black water. "Someone fell off."

"Yeah, maybe."

"Maybe? Well what else could it be? Some damn fool tripped and fell in and drown. I damn near did it myself last night."

"Yeah," Tyler said again, softer this time, "maybe."

20

Sleep had finally come in the hours before dawn. But with the sun up and people talking, Will couldn't sleep any longer. Though the amount of talk had greatly diminished since the first day out here. Odd how the body did that, he thought. Just knew how to preserve its strength in times of emergency.

Elizabeth was up. She was at the helm with Bixby, and the big man was showing her how to steer the ship and pointing to the different sails and lines. Tyler, who was now asleep, looked terrible. His lips were cracked and bleeding, his eyes sunken in from lack of sleep with dark circles underneath them, and his hair matted up like a dirty rug. But the strains of the sea didn't seem to affect Elizabeth. She was laughing and, despite how dirty her dress was, appeared as lovely as ever.

That was the strength of women, he thought. They were much tougher than men. When men chose a mate, they only looked at the surface. At the appearance, which was the part of a person that faded the quickest with age. But he didn't believe that's what women looked at.

A man could be missing a limb, or be hideously ugly, or dumb as stone, and a woman wouldn't care. As long as he gave them his honest feelings. If he gave them what he felt inside, women wouldn't care about the rest. But that part in a man was the hardest to give over to someone else. It was the part that he protected from everything and everyone. The thing he didn't show to anyone else.

Mostly because a man was embarrassed he had it. A man was not supposed to have a soft spot like that. But he also didn't show it because he didn't want it to be hurt. A man didn't really know how someone else would react when he showed it to them.

Will wanted to show that side of himself, that side that had been buried deep inside of him, to Elizabeth Davenport.

Will stood and strolled across the lifeboat to the helm. Elizabeth saw him, smiled and waved. He smiled back, placing his hand against the wooden pole holding the sail. "Having fun?" he said.

"The lieutenant was just showing me how they navigate a ship. It's quite fascinating. Did you know that we have rafts? Two of them. So even the emergency vessels have emergency vessels. They thought of everything."

"Everything except water."

Bixby looked up to the sky. The sun was in and out, covered by black-gray clouds and then released a moment later. "Rain'll come soon enough," Bixby said. "Don't have to wait out here long for a storm."

Elizabeth trotted to Will as though they were in a park on a sunny day, rather than stuck at sea. She took his hand in hers and kissed him on the cheek. "I'm glad you're up."

"You seem happy," he said.

"Just excited to be alive I think. After how many people lost their lives... I think I'm just happy to be alive."

Will turned his eyes back to Bixby, who was watching one of his crew count the number of rations again. They'd done this every morning and evening. Will had no doubt that the punishment for sneaking extra rations would have been swift and brutal.

"Bixby, how many people were on this raft when we started?"

"What'dya mean when we started?"

"I mean when the *Britannia* was sunk, how many boarded this raft?"

"Why?"

"Because I think one of them is missing."

Bixby eyed him a moment in silence, then looked out over the lifeboat and counted. Will could tell he was counting because he was using his fingers. He got through all his fingers, and then all his fingers again on his left hand. Fifteen. But he counted again and then asked the person that was calculating the rations to tally how many people he saw. The man looked puzzled but did as he was asked.

"Fifteen, Lieutenant," he said.

Bixby grabbed Will's arm and pulled him aside at the helm. Far enough away so no one could hear what they were saying. "You need to keep your mouth shut about this."

Will pulled away, facing the big man square, though the top of his head only came to Bixby's throat. "If you ever touch me like that again, I'll break your hand."

Bixby chuckled. "You got piss in ya, I'll give you that, Yank."

Will, the anger bubbling within him, calmed himself. His father had told him that whenever he needed to calm down, he need only think about his mother. Once, a long time after his father's death, Will was being taken advantage of by a buyer. Will was desperate, down to his last two dollars, and badly needed the sale. But the buyers kept finding things wrong with the gun. The barrel was too long, or it didn't hold enough ammunition, or it felt rough in their hands. They informed him that they could find better quality weapons elsewhere.

Will had already gone down fifty percent in price, and they kept haggling with him. He was desperate and frustrated, and it came out as anger. Out of nowhere, what his father had said came to him. To think of his mother. And he did. He refused the sale and walked away.

He thought his mother had been a beautiful woman, though he wasn't sure if that was true or not. All mothers were beautiful to their children. Yet he remembered her as beautiful. Dark hair that went past her shoulders with pink lips and bright white teeth. She would laugh a certain way that he had never forgotten and, sometimes, in his dreams, he would hear her laughing.

As the anger seeped out of him like poison, Will relaxed and took a step back, putting some distance between them. "Why can't we tell anyone else?"

"Because the difference for these people between surviving and not is morale. If you hurt that, you hurt their chance'a livin' through this. It hurts morale if we go tellin' 'em people are missing."

Will looked back to Elizabeth who was standing at the side of the boat looking over the water. "What do you think happened?"

"Who the hell knows? People fall over and drown all

the time. Sometimes they go mad and jump over."

"We'd only been out here a day."

He shrugged and turned back to the helm. "People are odd that way."

The lifeboat seemed to be making progress. They had a good wind that filled the sails and pulled them along, that would whip their faces with heat when the sun was out and with icy frost in the dead of night. Will was amazed at the difference between night and day at sea. He had walked through the deserts of Utah and knew that temperatures in deserts dropped to near freezing without any wind or snow. But he didn't know the same was true for the ocean.

He lay by the stern, between Elizabeth and Tyler again. Tyler had been asleep for almost eight hours. He woke up for his meal only because Will forced him to. He ate about half of it and then lay back down. With no water for almost three days, food was getting difficult for him to get down as well. Hopefully, Bixby had announced to everyone, they would have rain tonight. As a precaution, they had dumped the contents out of all the plastic chests and left them at the bow with their lids open. Hoping they could fill them with fresh water.

It wasn't Will's watch, but he was awake anyway. The moon was covered entirely tonight, and the clouds blocked the stars. An eerie blackness came over the sea then. Something like standing in a dark room where, from somewhere you couldn't see, a little light was still coming in. There was enough light for him to see down the lifeboat and the faces of the people, but the water was black as oil.

The only sound he had heard for the past couple hours were the soft swells against the wood of the boat and the occasional splash of the sharks. The sharks were always there, in daylight and night. He didn't know why or how they knew that the people in the lifeboats were edible, much less that they were in trouble, but they never left.

He suddenly became aware that he hadn't heard any of the sharks for quite a while. He lifted himself, amazed at the effort just such a small action took when one was starving and dehydrated, and looked over the side.

The sea was silent. No fins anywhere he could see. He looked over to the man that was on watch. It was a passenger from the *Britannia*, not one of Bixby's crew. The man was sitting on the edge of the bow, whittling some small piece of wood or plastic with a knife.

He stared at the man whittling. He could hardly see him. Nothing more than an outline. But it was somehow comforting to watch him. The repetitive actions he was making with his hands and wrists. The way one foot was crossed over the other. The man was balding but had the rim of hair that was left around the temples. Or at least, that's how it looked in the dark. Truth was, Will couldn't make out his features at all, and he wondered how much of what he was seeing was created by his own mind.

As sleep began drifting over him, like grains of sand that started at his head and floated down over his skin to his feet, he kept his eyes on the man, wondering if the man was making a gift for someone. And if he'd survive long enough to get it to them.

21

Captain Philmore Reeves was in his cabin when a seaman knocked and said, "Sir, we're here."

Reeves swung his feet out from the bed. He was still in his boxers and an undershirt. He sat up and rubbed the sleep out of his eyes before he turned to the little bedside stand he had. A bottle of whiskey, half-empty, was sitting there like some beautiful Siren. He opened the top and drank down several gulps before replacing it and standing up.

He found his uniform crumpled in a heap in the corner and slipped it on. A small sink and mirror were off to the side of the cabin, and he checked his hair and splashed some water on his face before heading out.

The ship, the *Aurora*, was a rescue vessel. But it didn't look like a rescue vessel. Massive guns were mounted fore and aft, and the crew weren't dandies. They were hardened men who had spent months at sea. Men for who the land was now uncomfortable.

Reeves strode up the metal stairs onto the deck. The sun was high and the ocean appeared dark blue. He first went to the port side and leaned against the railing and watched the water. When he was a kid, the sea seemed as far away as the moon. He grew up right in the center of the United States in Kansas and had only seen pictures of the world's oceans. He didn't see the Atlantic until he was eighteen years old. And by then, he had thought correctly, the fascination would fade and this would become just another job. But every once in a while, the beauty of it all hit him. And he had to take a moment and stare at it.

When he was done, he drew in a big breath and let it out slowly through his nose. He loved the sea air. The way it filled your nostrils with salt. He looked out past the horizon and then turned and headed to the bridge.

His mate, Henry, was already there, surveying some maps. A thermos with a few empty cups was on the counter and Reeves took a cup and filled it with coffee from the thermos.

"What do you have?" Reeves asked, taking a sip and walking over to the maps.

"Should be half a klick west."

"A klick? This isn't the army you know."

"Sorry. Bad habit I picked up from my brother in law."

"How's he doing by the way?"

"Over in France. Doesn't hate it. Doesn't enjoy it, but doesn't hate it. Get a letter from him every month or so."

Reeves drank down some coffee. It was lukewarm and bitter. "Well, take us over half a *klick* and let's see what we got."

Reeves marched out to the deck and looked west. As the ship rolled through the waves, he began to see what he was looking for.

Debris would float by. Nothing large, not yet anyway,

but enough to know that something happened here.

Bits of clothing, ice chests, cups and several dozen other things floated around. A ship had sunk here, and these were the remnants. Reeves went to the railing and looked over. He scanned the area as far as he could see. There was no sign of survivors. But he knew there had to be some. There were always some.

Henry came out and joined him on the deck. “So, what should we do, sir?”

“There’s lifeboats out here. Let’s keep scanning.”

“Which direction?”

“Whichever way the currents were going yesterday.”

22

It wasn't clear who felt it first, but Will knew it wasn't him. He knew that because, in his hazy sleep, he heard someone shout, "Rain!"

He opened his eyes just as he felt the first few droplets. It was morning, the sky blanketed in dark clouds, thunder rumbling restlessly beyond. Tyler was sitting straight, facing the group at the bow. It was so different from the position Will had last seen him in that it startled him at first, particularly since Tyler wasn't blinking or moving.

Everyone was around the chests, arguing over the best position to leave them in to collect the most rain. As they argued, the rain fell faster, pelting boat, flesh and sea. Elizabeth was roused. Rather than cowering, she chuckled and opened her mouth, letting the droplets hit her tongue.

Will rose and made his way to the chests. They were filling quickly. One man tried to reach in for a taste and Bixby slapped him in the face so hard, the man flew back.

"No one drinks until we ration it," he bellowed.

Will looked up to the darkened sky and opened his own mouth. The rain didn't taste like rain in California. Here, it was clean and had the scent of the open ocean. He waited until he had a mouthful and then swallowed. The water went down smoothly and coated his parched throat. He hadn't realized how thirsty he was until that drink. And now he couldn't get enough.

He stood in that position a long time, drinking down four mouthfuls of water until he noticed that the chests were about half full. Bixby took a cup and dipped it in. He drank first. Then he shouted for everyone to form a line.

There, lined up in front of plastic chests that just saved their life, everyone got one cup of water. The best drink they would ever have in their lives. Will ambled back to the stern and sat, his belly filled with water for the first time in four days. It made him nauseated but it was a nausea he didn't mind. As long as he didn't vomit and lose everything he'd taken in.

Tyler hadn't risen to get in line and Elizabeth had to take a cup back to him. He drank it, but didn't say anything. Will had never seen him like this. He was usually upbeat. Ever the optimist, he bubbled with energy. The sullen, defeated creature in front of Will didn't even resemble his friend.

"Tyler," he said, leaning close to him so he could hear over the rain, "I'm worried about you."

He chuckled and looked at him. Tyler's eyes looked different. Distant; like he was observing everything from afar. "We're all gonna die here, Will. We're not gonna make it to Brazil."

"Don't be ridiculous. We got food, and now we got water, it's just a matter of time. We'll get there eventually."

He shook his head, turning his eyes back to the people at the bow. "There's fourteen now. Count them."

Will looked over the men. Everyone was up front. With water in them, they were even speaking to one another, something they hadn't done all day.

He counted, starting with Bixby. He got the group... eleven. With the three of them, that was fourteen.

"I'm right, aren't I?" Tyler said. He laughed. "We're gonna die out here, Will."

"Hey," Will said, grabbing him by his shirt. "We are not going to die. Stop saying that."

Will was angry and frustrated at the anger. Tyler didn't deserve it. He let go of his shirt and tried to figure out what was making him so angry. The only thought that kept coming to him was that he was afraid. And his response to the fear was anger.

"Sorry," Will said.

Tyler ran his hands through his hair. He looked up to the sky and closed his eyes, inhaling a deep breath, letting the rain pelt him on one side of his face and then the other. When he finally exhaled his breath, he looked at Will. A glimmer of the old Tyler was there. A sparkle in the eyes, a gesture, maybe. And as quickly as it had come, it was gone. And the melancholy, or whatever the hell it was, returned.

"We're not going to survive this, Will."

"People are falling overboard. Or maybe someone's throwing them off. Either way, I think one of us should be up at all times."

He shook his head slowly, watching the people at the bow again. "No, that's not what it is. We're not alone out here."

23

The rain stopped as quickly as it had come, but the chests were filled two-thirds of the way. Enough, Will guessed, for one cup of water a day for each person on board for three days. But probably no more than that.

And as the clouds cleared and the sun poked through the sky again, revealing a brightness that made Will squint, several men were baling the rainwater from the boat into the chests. Some would take sips before tossing it in. Others would dump it over their heads, letting it slide down their bodies to their feet.

Bixby announced that they had underestimated their food stores and that they could add another spoonful of condensed milk to their daily rations. They would have one spoonful in the morning and the biscuit and jerky at night with the other spoonful. Some of the people used wooden spoons they'd found in the chests, and the Brits on board took the milk dry without mixing it with water. Will received his in a cup mixed with half a cup of water, half his daily allowance. The milk tasted watered down, and bits of powder still swam in the mixture, but overall it was good. And it relieved an aching belly long enough to hold out for the evening food.

As Will was walking back from the bow to the stern, he saw a man lying on his side. His legs and arms were severely sunburned. Thick blisters covered his exposed flesh, filled with a thin, white fluid.

"What's your name?" Will said, leaning over the man.

"Henry," he said, his voice hardly a whisper.

"Henry, you've got some bad blisters right here."

"I know."

"Can you do anything about them?"

He closed his eyes and shook his head softly. Will wouldn't have noticed if he wasn't staring right at him. "Do you want me to do something?"

"I don't care."

Will rose and finished the rest of his milk before placing the cup by the chests to be used by others. He saw the supplies piled up near the helm, just behind Bixby. Will walked over to the big man who was busy playing with something in his hand and staring out over the water.

"That man's got bad blisters."

"So?"

"So I need to drain them. After that, he might get an infection. I need bandages."

Bixby turned away from the sea and stared at him. "You want I waste bandages on some damned blisters?"

"He needs it. They could get infected like this, too. And we wouldn't even notice."

Bixby exhaled loudly and threw him a small package of bandages and a folded knife. Will took the knife, opened it up, checking how large the blade was, and then closed it again. As he was about to turn away, he saw what Bixby was playing with: A small wooden toy. Something that you might whittle down from a larger piece of wood.

"Where'd you get that?" Will asked.

"This? I found it on the deck. Yours?"

Will looked around to the men and realized who it was that was missing. "There was a bald guy on watch last night. Had a rim of hair around his head but completely bald up top. He was making that while sitting at the bow."

"Yeah, well, he can have it back."

"Thing is, he's not here."

The two men were silent a moment. The big man walked over and counted everyone again, using his fingers as he had last time. He counted once more, and then once more after that. "Bullocks."

"I don't think it's likely that two people fell overboard in succession. Do you?"

He looked to him, his eyes narrowing to slits. "What're you gettin' at?"

"I think someone threw those men over. I don't know why. Maybe to make the rations for the rest of us last longer."

"Someone, huh? Someone like me ya mean?"

"I didn't say that."

"You didn't have to." Bixby walked toward him, towering over Will's lithe frame. "You got somethin' to say to me, you say it to my face like a man."

"Okay," Will said. "If not you, then someone on your crew threw those men over. I understand that it increases our chances of survival, but that's not the way to do it. You knew no one would approve, so you do it at night when we're all asleep."

He grinned. "If I was doin' that, you'd be the first one over."

Will didn't flinch. He didn't step away or move. But he also didn't have a retort. He knew it was true. Bixby wouldn't lose a second of sleep if he tossed Will into the Atlantic and left him alone at sea.

"You wanna know something queer?" Will said. "I actually believe you."

"Good."

"So," Will said, looking back over the men, "then that means it's someone else."

"Aye, so it does."

"What're we gonna do?"

"Nothin'."

"Nothing? Really? Someone's killing people and we're going to do nothing?"

"We're gonna watch and see what happens."

"See what happens when someone else loses their life, you mean."

He shrugged and sat back down, returning his eyes to the ocean and his hands to fidgeting with the toy. "We don't know what it is. I'll have two on watch tonight and we'll see what happens. And I think you just volunteered for the first shift."

By midday, boredom had sunk in. Will, and he guessed everybody else, was too exhausted to do anything about it. It was a kind of exhaustion that Will could see someone lying down from it and just never getting up again. It permeated his bones, making them feel like they could snap if he stood up. He never wanted to move again.

But the problem was if he lay too long in any one position, he began to get sores. These in addition to the sunburns.

So people got up and tossed around and walked the length of the lifeboat, but tried not to speak. As though that were the difference between having energy and not.

"Will," Elizabeth said, "do you ever wish you had children?"

"I do."

"I bet a lot of people don't want children. But I'm glad to hear you're not one of them. I want lots of children. As many as I can have. But life just never put me in a place I could do it."

"You're still young. You should enjoy life as much as possible before you run off and settle down."

She was silent a moment. "I don't know if that's going to happen now."

"Elizabeth," he said, turning toward her, "it's been five days. Just five. People are sometimes stuck on the ocean for weeks before they get rescued or hit land. Besides, we're making progress every day."

The words neither felt sincere coming out, nor did they have the desired effect of comforting her. They felt like hollow, empty words. The words you'd tell a child hiding under their bed from monsters. But Elizabeth was kind enough not to mention it. Instead, she reached over and took his hand and said, "Well at least I have you with me. I think I'd go mad with these barbarians."

"Barbarians? The other day you were all giggles with Bixby."

"He seems all right. But some of these men stare at me like I'm a side of beef."

Will hesitated. "Elizabeth, I'm going to tell you something that I don't think too many people on this lifeboat have paid attention to."

He told her about the disappearances and about Bixby's plan to have two on watch and see what happens. She didn't say anything in response other than "Be careful." Almost like she was expecting news like this and it didn't surprise her.

After their meal, Will stood and walked the length of the lifeboat several times. He really didn't have the energy or the inclination, but he did it anyway. He needed to keep moving. The movement was a sign of life.

He walked a total of maybe a hundred feet before his legs burned with fatigue. He sat back down on the transom, and none of them spoke as night fell.

Elizabeth slept after the sun had set, but Tyler remained awake. Will could see the other watch for tonight near the bow. He decided it'd be best for the two of them to be closer to each other and he crossed to the bow.

"You the other watch?"

"Yes," the man said. He was Indian with a Hindi accent mixed with a British accent. Giving it an odd accentuation Will had never heard before.

Will sat down, his hands on his knees, and surveyed the rest of the people on the boat. The sky was clear and the moon was out again, so he could see all their faces. He was trying to make out the face of a murderer. But he had seen so many murderers in his life the one thing he knew about them was that they could be anyone. They had no defining characteristics.

The Indian was sitting on the edge of the boat. His arms were folded and he was looking out over the water.

Not taking it in, just passively observing. He was silent and Will didn't get the impression he was in a talking mood.

Up at the helm, Bixby was snoring like a bear. Will looked at him, watching the big man's belly go up and down in long waves. He heard splashing and assumed the sharks were back. When he looked over to the Indian, the man wasn't there.

Will looked down toward the stern and then back up at the helm.

The man wasn't there.

Will was on his feet and rushed to the side of the vessel where the man had been sitting. The water spread frothy waves outward like someone threw a stone in a pond. Other than that, nothing. He leaned farther over the side, staring down into the blackness.

No movement, no cries for help or frantic clawing for air. Nothing but an unnerving silence.

The man was just gone.

Will backed away from the edge. Without looking behind him, he tripped over the foot of another man and stumbled backward. He would have gone right over the side of the lifeboat if he hadn't caught himself with both hands. He straightened up, staring out over the sea—a breeze blowing his hair and cooling his sunburnt skin.

Tyler was right. They weren't alone out here.

24

Sometime before daybreak on the eighth day, the main halyards broke, causing the sail to drop. Bixby and his men went to work. An exhausted, starved crew. Will rose and went to help them, but stopped. He had attempted to sleep at the stern, his arm around Elizabeth, his foot resting on Tyler's leg. He wanted to be able to tell if they moved at all in the night. But sleep had been impossible, and he just stayed up.

Every small splash sent a jolt through him. It brought up images of every horrible thing that had ever been hiding under his bed or in his closet as a child. Rows and rows of monsters danced through his mind. Of all the horrible ways he could die out here, underneath the surface of the ocean in the cold, black depths was the worst.

As the men went about to fix the halyards, Tyler was up. He had grown weaker. He pushed himself up on his hands and leaned back against the transom. Neither of them spoke for a moment as the sun broke over the horizon and sunlight began pounding down on them again.

"I... I think I saw something," Will said softly.

Tyler tilted his head toward him. "What?"

"I don't know. The other man on watch a few days ago... he's gone. He was there one second and was gone the next. No one would've had time to throw him over. And he didn't make a single noise like someone would've if they'd fallen in. His head never broke the surface. He just... disappeared. I didn't say anything because I thought I was hallucinating. But I know I'm not now."

Tyler moved his head forward again. "Have you told anyone else?"

"No."

"They won't believe you. They'll think maybe you killed him."

Will nodded. "I thought that, too. Especially Bixby. I think he's looking for an excuse to toss me overboard."

"You can't say anything then. Let them figure it out for themselves."

"But what... I mean, what could do something like that? I thought maybe a shark leapt up and nabbed him, but he would've screamed, or swore or made some noise. Something."

"I don't think it was a shark."

"What then?"

He shook his head. "I don't know. But I..."

"What?"

"I think we've got company."

Will looked up to see a man standing over him. An older man with gray hair cropped short. He was chewing on a small bit of wood and he stared at Elizabeth as she slept. He finally looked to Will and said, "The Lieutenant wants to see ya."

"Well tell him to come ask me."

The man stared at him a bit, and then turned around

and walked back, glancing once more to Elizabeth.

It was only a matter of time, Will thought. How long could these men resist a beautiful woman in their midst? How long until they realized there were no police and Will was her only protector? They could toss him and Tyler out of the vessel and do whatever they wanted with Elizabeth. Right now, they were still fresh out to sea. But at some point, Will knew, the restrictions of civilization would seem like a fading memory.

Bixby was bent over the sail as the older man told him something. Bixby looked up and stomped across the lifeboat, coming for the stern. A tool, a wrench or something, was in his hand as he towered over Will.

"This is my vessel," he bellowed loud enough for everyone to hear. "When you're on my vessel, you come when I tell you to come."

"If you want to speak to me, come speak to me. Don't call me over like a dog."

Bixby leaned down, so close Will could smell his stinking breath. His teeth were yellow, all except his right K9, which was black with rot. "Maybe you are a dog and that's how I treat ya?"

Will said nothing. Now was not the time to have it out. Not with all these men watching him. Bixby had at least half a dozen of his former crew that seemed to do everything he asked. Aside from them, there were only three passengers, and Will, Elizabeth and Tyler. Six passengers and seven crew. And there was no guarantee that any of the crew would come to Will's aid should he and Bixby come to blows. And Tyler certainly wasn't in any condition to help. The odds were that Will would face Bixby and his entire crew completely alone. So he held his tongue.

Bixby grinned, sensing his victory. He stood up straight and said, "Need ever' able-bodied man helpin'."

Will rose and followed him to the sails.

The work was backbreaking. Other leaks had sprung and several men were busy baling water out of the lifeboat. Two of them were working on the sail, with Bixby checking over all the work done.

Will was put on the bales. He used one of the empty cups. One cupful at a time, he dumped out the transparent liquid into a vast field of blue. Blue as far as he could see in any direction. If he looked up close, the water had a greenish tint. And he didn't know enough about the sea to know why.

It seemed for every cupful that went out, another two came in. The leaks were springing everywhere now, and there was talk of permanent crews on bale duty. That seemed an impossible scenario. The exhaustion that had set in would make the work so difficult the men couldn't do it for more than a few minutes at a time. But that wasn't the main thing he worried about.

The water had lasted less than half the time they thought it would. Bixby had miscalculated. They should have had half a cup a day for each man. At one cup a day, the chests were nearly empty. And there wasn't a cloud in the sky.

Will baled until his arms burned so intensely he couldn't lift them anymore. Not even to wipe the sweat off his brow. By midday, he had nothing left and had to hand the cup off to someone else. At this point, he had stripped down to just his trousers, his feet waterlogged from standing directly on the soaked deck. At least three inches of water was permanently a part of the ship now. And no matter how much the men baled, it didn't seem to go down. He wondered if they'd have to bale through the night as well.

By the evening meal, he couldn't even lift the food to his mouth. Elizabeth was feeling the effects of the last few days as well. She wasn't speaking and her lips were dry and cracked. She wolfed down her food before realizing that they could only have a couple of sips of water each. Will, despite desperately needing to replace the moisture he lost baling water, gave his portion to her.

And when night fell, the watch had been divided. One trend Will had seen was that Bixby's crew wasn't assigned watches very much. It was almost exclusively the three other passengers and Will and Tyler. Tyler was in no shape to do anything, so Will would stay up for both their shifts.

He wanted to see what it was they were facing anyhow.

25

Several days passed in a hazy stupor. During the day, Will would work for a few hours baling water. The length of time he could do it shortened every day. And even Bixby's hardened crew couldn't function well anymore. They would lay about all day and the only time they rose was for a bit of food, which had been reduced again to one spoonful of condensed milk and a bit of jerky every night because they had run out of biscuits. When something was wrong with the halyards or sails, they would rouse themselves enough to repair it and then go right back to lying in the exact spot they had been in before.

After a particularly brutal session of baling that lasted what seemed like hours, Will limped back to the stern and collapsed against the transom. Elizabeth was staring off at the sea, squinting from the intense sunlight. A salty breeze was blowing and her hair moved with it.

"Something terrible's going to happen, Will. I can feel it. I felt it when I got on the *Britannia*, and I feel it now."

He couldn't answer right away. It took too much strength to talk. So instead he closed his eyes and looked up to the sky, taking a moment to catch his breath. “Something terrible’s already happened. We’re stuck on this damn boat.”

When enough strength had returned to him that he could actually move, he looked out over the lifeboat and counted the men.

Nine.

Over the past several days, the night watch was disappearing. Everyone had noticed, had probably noticed long ago. But no one said anything. Will brought it up once to Bixby but all the big man said was, “Ain’t my concern if people wanna go jumpin’ overboard.”

It was incredible the human capacity for denial. Every person on that lifeboat knew something was in the water. Something was following them around and only striking at night, but no one talked about it. They still referred to the missing as though they had decided to jump ship themselves, which wasn’t entirely fanciful.

Yesterday, one of the crew had drank seawater. He gulped it down quickly, before anyone could stop him. But that evening, he was acting like a lunatic. Ranting about people he must’ve known in his past, about presidents and kings that he was friends with, about a wife that he couldn’t describe. He was one of Bixby’s crew, and several men tried to calm him down, to lay him by the helm and give him a bit of water to soothe his stomach. But he fought them off like a lion.

He bashed one in the face so hard, the man’s teeth went flying into the water. Then the man, still ranting, leapt overboard.

There was no attempt to rescue him. Everyone understood it wouldn’t do any good, and even Will didn’t fight for the man. He didn’t have the strength. Everyone just watched as the swells would pull the man under and he would come up gurgling and gasp for air. Every second, he drifted farther and farther from the lifeboat, until he was nearly out of view. And then, he was just gone.

The incident had stayed with Will. Though it wasn't Bixby's fault, Will attributed the death to him. He didn't know why, but every misfortune was attributed to him right now. Perhaps a coping mechanism so he wouldn't have to think about the randomness that truly caused him to be here—dying on a bit of sinking planks with something in the water pulling them to their deaths.

Bixby's crew had been reduced to five not including Bixby. The three passengers were all gone. Only the crew, and themselves were left. Will reached down to his pocket and felt the folding knife Bixby had tossed him. He had never returned it.

As night fell, the demarcation line was clear. About the middle of the boat was an open space. Bixby and his crew were at the helm, Will and everyone else at the stern. The only problem Will saw with that was that the remaining food was at the helm. And darkness was falling. They should have been fed a long time ago.

Slowly, he rose. His legs felt like sticks that could break just by putting weight on them. He had to take a moment and steady himself. He looked at Elizabeth, who was drifting in and out of sleep, and Tyler, who had been asleep nearly the entire day: or at least didn't have the strength to open his eyes. He looked sicklier than ever. Emaciated with a dull, gray pallor. His lips were like peeled grapes that hadn't been peeled all the way. Ragged bits of skin hanging off and getting into his mouth.

Will hobbled over to the bow and stood before Bixby

and his men. Bixby didn't look that emaciated. Not like everyone else. It could've been because he was naturally a big man and had a lot of extra fat and muscle on him. But it could've been something else as well.

"We haven't been given our rations," Will said.

Bixby looked at him. "You didn't work that much today. You get rations when you work. And them other two is just taking up space."

Will felt like that was a threat. He wouldn't have been surprised if his men would've stood and faced him. The one advantage he had was that they were just as tired, if not more so, than him. No one looked well, and he guessed because they'd worked more hours today than he had, they probably felt worse.

"I can go without mine," Will said, "but I want the rations for Elizabeth and Tyler."

"And what you gonna do if I say no, Yank?"

Will stood still. A few of the men scoffed, thinking him a coward no doubt. He didn't look at them. He kept his eyes on Bixby. "I'm going to wait until that thing in the water kills all of you and then I'm going to get the food myself."

None of the men moved or spoke. It had silenced them. They had denied to themselves what was happening, what exactly they were facing. They denied it because it was too horrible to even think about. But he'd brought it right to the surface for them to gaze at.

They were not the top of the food chain out here. And all of them knew it.

Will slowly made his way back to the stern and leaned against the transom. He looked at Tyler whose eyes were open, though he hadn't moved otherwise. "Afraid we won't be eating today," Will said.

"That's okay," Tyler said in a hoarse, quiet voice.

"I'll get you some food tomorrow, Tyler. Even if I have to dive into the ocean and grab some bastard fish myself."

"I don't need any."

Will, the anger blowing in him like a volcano, lashed out at his friend. He struck Tyler on the shoulder with a fist. "What the hell is the matter with you? You don't just give up."

Tyler didn't say anything for a long time. His eyes were open, and he was taking Will in, but it almost seemed like he was somewhere else.

"I think I know what it is," Tyler said.

"What *it* is?"

"Yes. It. My father's told me stories. He was in the Navy during the first war. He said there's things in the ocean we can't explain. That the ocean is so deep and vast that we don't know even a fraction of what's down there. And he said there's things that, every once in a while, come up. He doesn't know why they come up. If it's something we've done or if they're just curious. But they come up… they come up, Will. And we can't stop them."

"Like what kind of things?"

Tyler swallowed, though Will doubted he had any saliva left. "He would never talk about it specifically. He was in a raft for over a week when his transport ship was hit. The raft was overflowing with people, and so some of them had to hang off the sides. He said some mornings they would wake up and some of the men would be gone. Once, one of the men was cut in half. All in silence. Without even enough splashing to wake someone up that was right next to him." Tyler took a moment to catch his breath. "My father said there's evil things in the sea."

Will didn't respond right away. He held Tyler's gaze for a long time and then said, "That's bologna."

Elizabeth stirred next to him. She didn't look well. The dehydration had taken its toll, and her skin seemed to sag off of her bones. Her hair was falling out in patches. Not enough to be noticeable to anyone that wasn't sitting directly next to her. But it was there. And he didn't know if she noticed.

"No rations tonight?" she said.

"Afraid not. I'll get some in the morning though."

Elizabeth was silent a while. "We're going to die out here, aren't we?"

"I don't know," Will said. He had neither the energy nor the will to lie anymore. Every ounce of reserve he had was gone. He was running on fumes. Fumes and a dull hatred in his belly that said it was unfair for him to die and a man like Bixby to live.

"Will?" she said in almost a whisper.

"Yeah?"

"I don't want to be buried at sea. Don't bury me at sea. Wait until we get to land."

"You're not gonna have to be buried. We're gonna make it."

With that, they fell into a long silence. One that lasted hours, until the blackness of night covered everything.

Will knew he would be awake tonight, but it seemed no one on the lifeboat was sleeping. Whether from the pain of hunger or thirst, or the fear of what would happen if they closed their eyes. And Will had all of them.

He had felt intense hunger before, but not like this. For the past few days, it'd just been a general malaise. Something that would come in waves and then fade away. But now the hunger was acute. A stabbing pain in his belly that wouldn't go away and wouldn't fade. The thirst was far worse. Sharp aches in his sides and chest. Unlike the hunger, which could be remedied with a good meal, the critical thirst seemed to be doing permanent damage to his organs.

No one on the lifeboat was moving. Will could tell they were all awake, even Tyler and Bixby who usually slept through anything. No watch had been assigned tonight, probably because it was understood that no one would sleep.

The sound of the ocean, something Will had grown accustomed to by now, seemed new to him. Because of the fear that gripped his guts like a fist, all his senses were heightened. And things he would never have noticed in a reasonable state were now forefront in his attention. The way the breeze wisped as it tugged at the sails. A thump from a large swell on the side of the lifeboat, the way the moon reflected off the eyes of the other passengers in dim crescents of light.

Off in the distance, the mournful cry of a whale echoed through the sea. It rose and fell in pitch, the rhythm constant. It sounded almost human. Meaning was there, Will thought. It wasn't the random sound of rats or insects. The whale was communicating something that it had to get out.

And while he listened to the cries, another sound caught his attention. A light scraping. Like fingernails on wood.

At first, he thought someone was running their hands

along the wooden planks. But then the sound moved in position. It was moving from the bow to the stern in one long stride. The sound was coming from underneath the boat. Something was scraping alongside the bottom.

"Tyler," he whispered. "Tyler, wake up."

"What?"

"Something's underneath the boat."

Tyler, wordlessly, sat up. He leaned his back against the transom and scanned the water around them as best as he could from where he was sitting. "Are you sure?"

"It stopped."

The two men listened intently. But the sound wasn't there anymore. They watched Bixby and his men as they fought sleep away. Some of them had already succumbed and were snoring. Others were moving and slapping themselves to try to stay awake. Most of them were too exhausted to do anything but sleep until something woke them up.

Will looked at Elizabeth. He worried for her. The exposure to the elements and starvation seemed to be affecting her the worst.

"If we don't get in soon," Will whispered, "she'll die."

Tyler shook his head. "I think we'll probably be joining her."

26

The morning came like a welcome guest. Almost as soon as the sun had broken over the horizon and began to light up the sea, Will's spirits lifted. Sunlight had a propensity to do that.

He didn't move for a while. Just let the light burn away the darkness and wash over the boat, illuminating the men on the other end. Will glanced to Elizabeth, who still had the deep breathing of sleep, and then he was about to see if Tyler was awake when a scream shattered his calm.

A man at the bow was frantic, clawing at the other men, shrieking at the top of his lungs. Two other men grabbed him as he stood and all three fell over. Bixby ran down and flung the men off each other, and then he froze. They all did. Except the man that had been screaming. He dashed for the helm and tucked himself behind it.

Bixby was staring down at something. The men fell silent as though in awe or reverence. Will couldn't tell which. He pushed himself up, the effort taking so much of his energy he nearly collapsed. He fought through the pain and soreness and hobbled forward a few steps until he could see.

A human leg lay there, severed at the thigh. The cloth of the pants had been shredded to pieces, as had the skin and the flesh. Everything was torn right down to the bleached white bone. Bixby looked over his men. There were only four left. Someone else had disappeared in the night, the man that had been connected to that leg.

Bixby bent down and lifted the leg. He tossed it overboard without a moment's hesitation. Will watched as the leg drifted less than half a minute before the first fin circled it. Then another and another. The head of one shark, dull gray in the sunlight, popped up and bit into the thigh and pulled the leg beneath the surface. Other fins came near and then the sharks disappeared into the murky depths.

Will looked at Bixby, who glared at him but said nothing. The big man turned away and sat down. The other men returned to what they were doing, which was little more than staring off into space and wasting time.

Will sat back down.

"What was it?" Elizabeth asked, now awake.

"Nothing."

"Will, don't..."

He looked at her. Though her skin, hair, and clothing appeared ragged and beaten, her eyes still sparkled like jewels. He grinned a weak little grin in an attempt to comfort her. "It's nothing, really. Try and rest. I'm going to get you some breakfast."

Will needed a moment before he could stand up again. He felt winded, like he'd just run from one city to another rather than just standing and walking a few paces. He caught his breath the best he thought he could and then pushed himself up again. Looking down on Tyler, he could see that the screaming hadn't bothered him much. Or if it had, he didn't show it.

The bow of the ship seemed to take longer to get to now. Even though there were less people to climb over to get there. A permanent puddle of about five inches covered the deck and Will's feet swooshed through it.

The men didn't rise or look at him. Everyone was in their own world of pain and hunger.

Will stood before Bixby. "Elizabeth needs food."

"Well I hope she can fish 'cause that's the only way she's gettin' it."

Will leaned against the helm. "Give her some food you bastard."

He chuckled weakly. "No."

The knife in his pocket felt small suddenly. Even though he had felt it a thousand times and never noticed before. He pulled out the knife and unfolded it. Bixby didn't even seem to notice.

"And what you gonna do with that, Yank?"

"I'm going to kill you."

"If you got the strength, let's see it."

Will let the knife dangle in his fingers. He didn't threaten with it or even pretend to. He just let it dangle. The two of them stared at each other. Will knew he could kill him. Could slit the man's throat right there. In the past week, every misfortune that had fallen him, he'd attributed to this man. Bixby was now the personification of Will's own death. When Will looked at him, he didn't feel anger or remorse or even hatred. Just a dull regret.

"Give her some food," he said again. "I don't want to kill you, but I will."

Bixby sat up. "No," he said slowly, ensuring Will

heard him.

Will felt the weight of the knife in his hands. It was light but he knew the blade was sharp. A good knife meant for actual work rather than decoration. He sighed and turned to leave, Bixby chuckling.

In a flash of movement, Will flung himself at the big man. The two men toppled over. Will was on top, trying to wrap his knees around the big man's hips. One knee fell into place but Bixby was fighting the other one. Will lifted the knife but Bixby grabbed his wrist, preventing it from coming down into him.

Will pushed the knife but had no strength left. Even emaciated and starving, Bixby was the stronger man. He reached up and smashed Will in the face with his meaty palm. Then he hit him with a fist and Will saw stars. The knife fell out of his hand.

Will wrapped his hands around Bixby's throat, but it was too late. Two other men grabbed him, one on each arm. They hoisted him up. Will kicked and struggled. One arm got free and he slammed it into a man's nose, causing blood to cascade down over his chin before the man grabbed Will again.

Bixby stood up to his full height. He swung with a fist so hard, Will could've sworn he shattered his cheekbone. Bixby hit him twice. It didn't take much more than that. But the big man was exhausted, too. He might not have had anything else in him.

"Toss him over," the big man said.

"No!" Will shrieked. He fought against his captors, kicking at the boat for leverage. Pulling his arms away like a child trying to get away from a parent. The third man was on him, too. Everyone but Bixby, who hung back, trying to catch his breath and leaning against the side of the boat for balance.

The men brought Will toward the sea. Will managed to get one arm free and elbowed the man again in the nose. He stumbled back. Will broke free and attempted to dash to the stern, though he didn't know what would be there that could help him. But the stern was where he had been this entire cursed time. It was the only place that offered a little comfort to him.

He didn't make it there.

One of the men tackled him at the waist and they fell over, splashing into the water at the bottom of the vessel. The men then picked him up. Everyone was drained, but they had enough strength for one last push.

The men attempted to haul him overboard and Will let his legs collapse under him, becoming dead weight. The men nearly dropped him at first. Bixby shouted something akin to, "You'll be joining him if you don't get him over," and the men lifted Will.

He could see over the boat now, into the dark blue water. He was grunting like an animal, pushing with everything he had to stay on the boat, but he was losing.

And then the pressure eased suddenly. One of the men had let go. On the periphery of his vision, Will saw that the man had fallen over, hanging on to the boat with one hand. Tyler's face appeared and, like an animal, he bit the man's fingers. The man screamed, and let go. Splashing down into the water and sinking below.

Will had enough in him that, with the two men still hanging on distracted, he pushed them away. Tyler stood behind him trying to push them in as well. Bixby's men were sucking in air as though they were the ones drowning. They didn't put up as much of a fight. Not when they were evenly matched.

The man in the water had been the one Will had cracked in the nose. He was still bleeding.

"Help!" he screamed. "Help!" They were deep, guttural screams that turned to a high-pitched shrieking toward the end. The shrieks of someone that knew they were about to die.

The other two men didn't move. They looked to Bixby who was staring at the man in the water with a detached, curious look. Like he was observing some science experiment and didn't care which way it turned out.

The man was still screaming, but the swells would rise into his mouth and leave a wet, gurgled screech. Will watched him, too. He had no strength left to save the man and even if he could, he wouldn't. Bixby looked at Will with venom. And Will knew right then that only one of them would be allowed to survive this voyage.

The man in the water stopped screaming. Will looked at him. His face was pale, pure white almost, and his eyes were wide. He jerked backward, as though tied to a rope and being pulled. And then he jerked again. Then the screaming and hollering started, the pounding of the water. And the fins appeared.

Will had always thought a shark attack would be swift and silent. That they would pull their victim underneath the surface and finish them there. But that's not how it was. The fish were taking chunks out of the man. They would stealthily come up behind him, sink their teeth into his back or legs, and then violently thrash a moment. Coming away with a mouthful of bloody, ragged flesh.

They hit the man again and again and again. The man was now begging, pleading with the sharks to stop as though they cared. And the fish just kept coming. Until the man finally sunk underwater, popped up one last time, his face upturned to the sky, and was pulled down for good.

27

Will was at the stern again. The three men up at the bow now had all the food. The water had run out already, so they were all slowly dying of thirst, but the food was the only thing on Will's mind right now.

Elizabeth was delirious. She had been talking to herself in her sleep and she felt hot, like she was burning up with fever. Will dipped his shirt into the water on the deck and placed the shirt over her head.

Tyler was sitting upright against the transom. His eyes were only half-open as he passively watched the other men. No one spoke. No one needed to.

The water on the deck was now easily seven inches, but no one was trying to bale. It wouldn't have a made a difference; it was coming in much faster than they could've gotten it out. The boat would sink soon.

"Tyler," Will said, his voice hoarse.

"Yes?" he said after a second.

"There's only one raft. This boat's not gonna make it."

Tyler nodded. "I know."

Will had never been a violent man. He knew how to

fight, growing up where he did if a kid didn't fight he was a target. And he wasn't about to be anybody's target. But the thought of what they had to do to survive filled him with disgust. For them to live, the other three men had to die. And he knew those men were thinking the same thing about them.

Tyler mumbled, "How should we... I mean, how do we do it?"

"I think we wait for nightfall. I don't think we can take all three. That one there, with the red hair, let's get him. Toss him over. We're still probably outmatched on the other two but it'll be close to a fair fight."

The man with the red hair was younger, maybe twenty-three or twenty-four. He was sitting hunched over, staring at the water pooling around him. His skin was dirty and his fingernails were nearly black. His face was sunken in from starvation and lack of sleep. He was drifting in and out of consciousness. He was weak, and everyone knew it. He also happened to be sitting closest to the stern.

The day dragged so slowly Will wasn't sure he hadn't fainted and they had just moved into the next day. He felt every painful second, but his main concern was Elizabeth. She wasn't speaking anymore and just slept or lay there. Her skin was still hot and Will thought she might have sunstroke. She kept asking for water from the ocean, but he knew he couldn't give it to her. The one thing he knew for certain about being out on the ocean was that you couldn't drink seawater. Something to do with the salt shutting your kidneys down. So he doused her head with the lukewarm water as often as he could and tried to keep her shaded.

"I don't know if we're going to live," Tyler said softly.

Will was silent a moment. "Don't talk like that now."

"No, I want to do this. I want to tell you that I've done some horrible things, Will."

"You? What could you have possibly done that was horrible?"

He swallowed. "I've robbed men, I've stolen, I've womanized, gambled, fought—"

"Hell Tyler, if that's all you done you say hello to St. Peter for me. I done worse before I was even a man."

"There's more. I want to tell you. I need to tell someone before I die."

"I don't want to hear it. Just stop. Tell me when we get back."

The two men were silent for a long time. Will stared out over the dying sun as it fell into the ocean and wondered if this was the last sunset he would ever see. It was a good one. The sky painted pink and purple, the ocean reflecting a dim orange. If it was his last one, it wasn't the worst thing to see before dying.

"When I was first starting out," Will said, "I used to sell to anybody. I wasn't discerning about it. It didn't matter to me who you were. If you had the cash, I would get you the guns you needed. There were these two fellas once. Younger fellas. They came to me and said they needed Browning m1919s. Something that fired a lot of shots quickly. I told them that those were military guns and they'd be better off if they got Thompsons. So they wanted four of them. I got them four of the best Tommy guns you ever could find. Brand new. They were so happy. They paid in cash and I went off thinking I was the cat's meow. I'd made more money in one deal than my father made in a year." Will glanced over to Bixby and his men. They were staring at the sinking sun, too. "About a week later, there was a big hubbub about a bank robbery in town. These four men had gone in and killed everyone. Men, women, and one child that was at the bank with his mother. They just waltzed in and shot everyone and took off with the dough.

"The coppers caught up with them. About a month later when they tried to do the same thing to another bank. Two of 'em died but two were arrested and their faces were in the papers. It was the men I'd sold the Tommys to. I threw up when I read that story. Threw up right there all over the *Los Angeles Times*. I've never hated myself so much in my life."

Tyler didn't say anything, and night fell over them like a blanket.

28

In the blackness, Will tried to guess what time of night it was. Maybe eleven, maybe midnight. Time didn't hold the same meaning for him anymore. He couldn't decipher how long he would be sitting in a single spot. The only thing that told him time had passed at all was the pain he felt in whatever part of his body was making contact with the boat. His buttocks, legs or back.

He scanned the boat for a weapon, but there was nothing. Three oars, but they were up front. The knife, and that was about it. This would have to be done with fists.

"Are your ready?" Will said, staring at Bixby's hulking mass as he was lying flat on his back, snoring.

Tyler nodded in the dark.

Will stood up and glanced at Elizabeth, who was moaning in her sleep. He didn't know how much longer she had. The water in the boat was almost a foot now, coming up about mid-calf. The bow was lower than the stern and had larger pools gathered. Stealth would not be something they would have on their side. Whenever anyone moved on the boat, they had to slosh through the water.

Will went first. He got all the way up to the bow, but didn't stand too close to the men. The two of them looked up and Will noticed that Bixby wasn't sleeping. He was staring up at the sky.

"You want to die now," Bixby said, "Yank?" He spit out *Yank* with such venom that Will knew there was no turning back. They would have it out right now and one way or another it would be settled.

"I didn't want this," Will said. "I just wanted some food for her."

"The woman can't work. She don't get no food."

"That's inhuman."

"No," he said, pulling himself up to a sitting position, "that's survival. You gotta make tough choices. You think I want to watch her die? I don't. But that's the choice you gotta make."

Will shook his head. "You made the wrong choice."

Bixby snarled like an animal and then made a move to rise. Will turned and jumped on the boy with the red hair. He had him by the legs. Tyler moved in and lifted him underneath the arms and they tossed him backward, over the side of the boat. The boy somersaulted into the water, shouting for help.

Bixby and the other man were up, but they didn't move in. Not yet. Bixby took out the knife. The other man grabbed oars and held them like baseball bats. Will took a few steps backward, pulling Tyler alongside him.

The man in the water was clawing at the boat now, trying to pull himself up. He realized it was impossible, so he started swimming toward the stern. Will knew he might be able to climb up on the transom and then they'd be boxed in on both sides. He couldn't let that happen.

They kept backing up with Bixby and his man taking steps forward. The splashing of the boy filled the air; jerky, panicked movements. Erratic, like a speared fish.

The boy made it to the back of the transom. If Will turned around to address him, he had no doubt Bixby and his man would rush in and he'd be the one in the water. But if he didn't, they'd take him out from both sides. Will quickly glanced back and saw the boy climbing up.

And then, just when he was almost in, the boy's eyes went wide and he froze. He grunted, something akin to having all the air knocked out of you all at once from a blow, and a thin strand of blood trickled down his lips.

The boy was holding on to a low pushpit and his fingers slipped off of it. His muscles gave out, and he collapsed onto the transom. Will could see something glistening about mid-waist. It was the boy's organs, flopping out into boat. He'd been torn in half.

Will turned to see if anyone else had seen it when he heard Bixby splashing through the boat. The big man swung with the knife. Will ducked, the blade going over his head, but it caught Tyler across the face. Tyler screamed as blood poured from the wound.

Bixby's man rushed forward… until he saw the young boy on the transom. Then the man's eyes went wide and he stood still. The oar fell out of his hand he was trembling so profusely. Slowly, he backed away.

Bixby swung with the knife again and again. All his effort directed at Will. But the big man was slow and telegraphed his swings by cocking his arm back to get more power. Will ducked and bobbed and stepped back to avoid the blade. But there was only so far he could go. The transom wasn't more than five feet behind him.

Will ducked low, coiling his legs to spring forward. He would have to take the blade somewhere and hopefully he could direct it to his shoulder or arm rather than in his chest or belly. Then he would have to take Bixby down. Maybe drown him in the water that was pulling the boat down into the sea.

Bixby lifted the blade to come in for another swing.

"A light!"

The two men stopped. It had been Bixby's man that shouted. He was pointing across the sea and shouting, "Light. Light!"

Will glanced to where the man was pointing. Not that far off was a single, dim light. A perfect circle of yellow. It was bouncing up and down with the swells and moving across the surface of the ocean. A ship.

"Hey!" Will bellowed. "Hey, over here, over here!" He waved his arms like a lunatic and tried to jump up and down, anything to get their attention even though it was pitch-black.

Bixby didn't move. He kept his eyes on the light for a long while and then shouted as well. Everyone was shouting except Tyler. His hand was covering his cheek, which was spilling blood over him, mixing with the water that was now knee-high.

"Hey!" Will screamed. The light was getting closer. It was a small vessel, probably, but he had no idea who it could be. He didn't know how far off from South America they were. It could be Brazilian, or it could've been German for all he knew. Though he would have preferred a prisoner of war camp to this.

The men shouted until they were hoarse. It appeared like the ship was heading directly toward them. But then, suddenly, as if banking hard to the left, the light disappeared. The men fell silent. They saw it again and shouted, but then it disappeared again. The boat was turning around.

"No!" Will screamed. "No, don't leave us. Don't you fucking leave us!"

But it was too late. The boat was gone.

"No!" he cried, kicking out at the water engulfing his legs. "No, no!"

He suddenly noticed that Bixby and his man weren't paying attention. The man was weeping, a soft quiet weeping where no tears came because he didn't have any to shed. Will, pulling up the last of his strength, rushed them.

He hit Bixby as hard as he could and the two of them went down. The knife flew out of his hand and plopped into the water in the boat near Tyler's feet.

"Get the knife!" Will shouted.

Tyler, one hand still covering his split cheek, bent down and searched the water for the knife with his other. He lifted it out of the water and held it in front of him. Will slammed his fist into Bixby's face several times, the big man trying to push him off but not defending himself.

Will stood up and looked to Bixby's man. He was still crying, his eyes fixated on the last place he'd seen the other ship. And as Will watched him, something he could never have imagined in his nightmares unfolded right before him.

The water next to the boat exploded in frothy waves. Something glistening and long, like a snake but as thick as a tree, thrust out of the water and wrapped itself around the man's head. It lifted him off his feet as though he were a mannequin and pulled him into the water so violently, he slammed right through the side of the ship, shattering the wooden planks.

Water rushed in. It was loud, like a waterfall, but only lasted a moment as the lifeboat filled with the sea. Will grabbed Elizabeth, holding her up as they sank. He wanted to run to the bow, but running was impossible now. He was swimming.

Near them was a large plank of wood, broken away when the man had been pulled in. Will, grunting, his head underwater because he didn't have the strength to tread, pushed her onto the wood. Then he lifted himself up, sucking in air as water splashed against his face. Tyler was there, too, and Will swam out and grabbed him. Bringing him back to the wooden plank, he suddenly felt the pull of the sinking lifeboat.

"Kick," he bellowed. "Kick now!"

They kicked, and though the progress was slow, they inched away from the boat. The vessel went down bow first, just as the *Britannia* had. Will glanced back exactly once and saw Bixby treading water, his face turned up to the sky and the ocean swells covering him a moment and then revealing him again.

"Keep kicking," Will said, turning away from the big man.

29

The exhaustion made his bones ache. Will felt it only as a distant pain as he slipped in and out of consciousness. When he was dimly aware that he was conscious, daylight had already arrived.

The wood was a large plank, about the size of a car. Probably not buoyant enough for all three of them to climb onto, but certainly enough to hang on. Elizabeth was clinging with most of her body on the wood. Her eyes were open and she was shivering, though nowhere near as bad as Will or Tyler.

On the opposite side of the wood, Will saw Tyler. He was white and trembling so badly his teeth were chattering. His lips were gray. They looked like two dead snails on his white face. Will could see his cheek clearly now. Though the bleeding had slowed, the cheek was cut in half. From the jaw muscle up to the nose. It was slowly trickling blood into the ocean.

Will tried to move and felt pain. In his legs, in his hips, in his back. Those were the most sharp, but his arms and shoulders felt like they'd been pulled out of their sockets, too. Everything hurt. So much pain radiated through him that he couldn't focus on any one part of it to determine what exactly needed his attention. So instead, he tried to think about other things. To focus on something else. The cold, or the sun burning his already sunburnt eyes. He'd noticed it a couple of days ago. Everything had a dim glow around it. Like fog. His eyes had been damaged from the constant brightness of the sun.

"Will," Tyler said through chattering teeth, "Wi— Will. I'm bleeding. I'm bleeding, Will."

"I know, Pal. Hang in there. Okay? You just hang in there."

"My leg really hurts. It really hurts, Will. I think it's broken."

Will straightened himself out, fire shooting up his back as his muscles stretched. "I'm sure you're okay."

"Can you check it, Will? Can you check if it's broken?"

Will hesitated a long time. The last of his strength had left him long ago. He had nothing left for Tyler. But still he moved down the scrap of wood. He came to his friend just as a swell rose and water got into his mouth. It made him gag and cough. When he stopped, he wiped his lips with the back of his arm. The water was warmer than it had been on the other side. Just as Will was wondering how that was possible, he noticed his own arm. The water rolling down his flesh was a light crimson.

A cloud of blood surrounded him. It was slowly dissipating, spreading out in all directions at once. Will pushed away slightly from the wood and looked into the water. He couldn't see anything but a red cloud. So he moved away from it, out of it, and then drew breath and dunked his head below the surface.

He looked at Tyler. His leg was missing from below the knee, spewing blood out from the wound. Around them, Will could feel movement. Not entirely close, not yet. But other creatures were there. The sharks had picked up the scent and were closing in.

He came out of the water. Tyler was shivering and could hardly speak, but managed to get out, "How's it look?"

"Fine, Pal. You're just fine."

"I don't think—I don't think I can make much use of the knife. My fingers won't move. Take it out of my pocket, would ya?"

As Will removed the knife from his friend's pocket, a soft sound whispered through the air. Will didn't recognize it at first. He tried to still himself so he could identify it. The sound occurred again and he knew what it was. Elizabeth. Her voice was hoarse, almost inaudible. He quickly moved himself near her. She gave him a weak grin. The difference between yesterday and today was pronounced. She looked like a different person. One that was now almost dead rather than dying.

"Will... he's bleeding, isn't he?"

Will swallowed, the traces of seawater in his mouth soothing his parched throat. "Yes."

"I heard him screaming. I heard him screaming that he was being eaten."

Will nodded. "He's lost a lot of blood."

"You have to let him go."

Will's brow furrowed. "What'd you mean let him go?"

"You know what I mean. He's bleeding into the water. You have to let him go."

He shook his head. "No. No, I won't do that."

"Then we'll all die, Will. We don't have the strength

to fight. We'll all die with him." Her eyes closed, and, for a moment, she seemed to be unconscious. With her eyes still closed she said, "You have to let him go so we can live."

He pushed himself away from her. He couldn't even look at her right now. How could she say something like that? Tyler was his friend. The whole reason Tyler was even out here was to make certain Will was all right. No, the possibility was too horrific even to contemplate. They would just float along with the currents like they had in the lifeboat. Eventually, they would hit land. They were headed the right direction. They just had to be patient...

Even as the words came to Will's mind, he didn't believe them. There was no happy ending to this. No way all of them were going to survive. They were all either going to die together, or be picked off one by one. Rationally, he had decided they should all just die together. That was the honorable thing to do. But something inside him wouldn't let him give up. Something deep in his bones that screamed to him a single word: *survive.*

His eyes gradually drifted to Tyler. The man was mumbling to himself, white as a ghost. Most of the blood in his body was gone, leaving a trail for the sharks.

No, Will thought. *I can't do it. I can't.*

Seemingly hearing his thoughts, Elizabeth mumbled, "Will, you have to let him go. Let him go."

Whatever it was inside of him that was screaming to survive was also screaming inside of her. They wanted to live, and their bodies had decided without any input from their minds that the only way to survive was to get as far away from Tyler as possible.

Will eased over to his friend. He put his arm around

him and emotion welled inside of him. He cried, though no tears came. And he thought of the man on the lifeboat, crying at the sight of a ship that should have been all their saviors. A ship that broke their hearts without even knowing it.

"I love you, Pal," he whispered.

"Will… you remember when, when we were in that hotel room with those two girls. They were actresses. And… the beautiful one with the blonde hair was drunk and kept wanting to go into the next room with you."

Will hesitated, leaning his head against Tyler's forehead. "Yeah, I remember."

"And… and I told you that I wanted her. And so I just took her hand and took her back into that room and left you with the other one. But you never said anything to me. You never said anything. Do you remember that?"

Will saw that Tyler's grip was loosening on the wood. He didn't have the strength to hold on. "Yeah, I remember."

"I always regretted that. I'm sorry, Will. I'm sorry I did that to you. I should've been a better friend to you."

Will couldn't look at him. He turned his head away, the pain rising in his gut up to his chest. He felt like vomiting, like weeping, like curling up into a ball and never coming out of it again. "You were always a good friend to me. The best a fella could have."

A thin smile came over Tyler's lips. Slowly, almost imperceptibly, Will removed his friend's hands from the wood. Tyler began to drift backward but didn't say anything. He still had the smile on his lips, his eyes turned to the sky as the scrap of wood, Will and Elizabeth went one way, and he drifted off in another.

Will dry heaved, but nothing came out. No fluid, no

food, nothing but pain. He looked up to Elizabeth who didn't seem conscious. But something gave away that she was. That she was fully aware of everything that was going on. Just a slight opening of her eyelids. And then, just as slowly as they had opened, they closed again.

Will heard splashing behind him, and a moan. Not really of pain. More like someone realizing the inevitable. Getting run over by it.

Will dry heaved again, and again, nothing came as the scrap of wood continued to drift away with the currents.

30

An alarm sounded somewhere, rousing Philmore Reeves. It was morning, he knew that much, but he couldn't guess as to the time. He knew the alarm; a man overboard signal. He jumped to his feet, threw on some clothes, and ran to the deck.

They'd been searching for days and came up with nothing. A few bits of debris here and there. The fact was, and they never told him this at the Naval Academy, but once someone was in the water more than twenty-four hours, their chances of survival dropped to near zero.

The ocean was too vast for rescue ships to find people. Particularly people that had been floating off with the currents for days at a time. But sometimes they would just happen across a boat or a raft with survivors. It was rare, but it was satisfying. Reeves knew every man on the *Aurora* saw themselves in those lifeboats and rafts. They all knew they could easily end up there, and they hoped like crazy that a ship like the *Aurora* would happen by for them.

Looking over the railing, Reeves saw his men pulling someone out of the water. A single male. He was a big man, scruffy looking, and clearly injured. But the boys got him up on deck and threw a blanket around him as someone went to fetch the doctor.

Reeves approached the man and bent down. "What's your name?"

"Lieutenant... Lieutenant Bixby of the SS *Britannia*, sir."

"Lieutenant, I'm Captain Reeves. You're safe now, son."

Bixby grinned, revealing yellow stained teeth. He laughed. Not chuckled, but actually laughed, and it caught Reeves off guard. The man was clearly delusional from too much sun and sea.

"Bixby, is there anyone else out here? Any other lifeboats you saw?"

Bixby hesitated a moment. "No, sir. I am the only survivor."

Something about the statement didn't sit right with Reeves. About the way Bixby looked when he said it. "You sure, son?"

"Yes, sir. I'm the only survivor of our lifeboat."

He nodded and rose. His first mate was behind him and said, "Shall we head back to port, Captain?"

"Yeah, I think we're done."

31

The ocean was so much colder than he would've ever thought possible. Will's teeth were chattering loudly and his hands trembled. It was an odd sensation, mostly because the sun was hot on his back. So he had the duel feeling of getting sunburnt while his body slowly froze as his core temperature dropped.

"It was the only thing we could do," Elizabeth said weakly.

"The man was my friend for years. I just tossed him away like he was nothing."

"Not nothing. We lived, Will. He died so we could live."

Somehow, the words weren't comforting.

The swells were low, which was the only thing saving their lives right now because neither one of them could kick to stay afloat. Every once in a while, something would float by that captured Will's attention. Once, he even saw a plastic bottle. Even out here in the middle of the ocean, garbage was still around.

"This reminds me of the plains," Will said through chattering teeth. "My daddy and me... we crossed the plains on foot. Sometimes we hitchhiked if there was roads. But in the plains there's nothing. Just vast open fields and then dense forests. I didn't know why we kept going. I thought we would stop and live there forever."

"I would love to see the plains. I've never been out of a city in my life. Except for this. And so far I think I'd like my money back."

Will grinned. He tried lifting himself up onto the scrap of wood, but it began to sink as soon as he put his full body weight on it. So he had to dangle in the water up to his chest. "I used to actually like the ocean."

She hesitated a moment, inhaling and exhaling several times before speaking again. Her speech was slow and seemed to take a lot of effort. "Will, what're we going to do when it comes back at night?"

"It was following the lifeboat, whatever it was. The lifeboat's gone now."

She shook her head softly. "No, it was following us."

An icy fear ran up Will's spine. Fear of the unknown. Of the darkness. He had the knife that Tyler had given him. He knew a quick way to end it. The femoral artery. He'd cut both, one in each leg, and bleed out into the water. He'd be dead before the sharks ever came. Quick fatigue would come over him, and he'd fall asleep and never wake up.

His grandfather had died the same way when he was a child; his father would always tell him stories about it. During the War of Southern Rebellion, his grandfather had been fighting in the forests of Virginia. The ammunition back then, Will's father had told him, wasn't like today where it cut through you. Back then, it was a solid metal ball that shattered everything in your body it touched.

His grandfather had been struck in the ribs and knew he was going to die. He could feel the bones loose near his heart. So he did two things: he made one of the privates under him swear that he would give something to his young son. A pocketwatch that was a family heirloom. And the second thing was that he took out his large hunting knife and stabbed into his femoral arteries in both legs.

When the private finally came after the war, he told Will's grandmother about what had happened. He said that he had died in less than two minutes by bleeding out and that it was peaceful.

Peaceful. That's all Will wanted right now. A peaceful death. A slow fading away from existence… anything but the constant dread that was eating up his guts.

"I think you can climb all the way on board this thing," he said. "Just stay on it as it goes with the currents."

Elizabeth looked at him. "That sounds like final advice."

He didn't respond.

"Will, this life and everything in it is out of our control. It's unpredictable. You could die, and five minutes later I could be rescued. You have to survive, for as long as you can. You have to survive. There's nothing else."

"I may not have any control over life, but I sure as hell can have some control over my death."

Elizabeth reached out, her fingers finding Will's hand. Though she was cold, she wasn't as cold as he was and her fingers felt warm against him. Somehow that warmth was enough. Gave him some glimmer in his mind that he needed to live. For what, he didn't know. But dying purposely by giving up wasn't an option.

"Please stay with me," she said. "I'm frightened."

He nodded. "I'll stay."

Neither one of them were bleeding. And they were motionless for hours. Will guessed they probably just looked and smelled like pieces of the wood from underneath. And because of that, there were no sharks anywhere. He didn't see a single fin... not until the sun began to set.

The first fin streaked across in front of them sometime in the early evening. It was small, belonging to a fish probably no bigger than three or four feet. But even a shark of that size could cut him open. And the only thing that would make their situation worse right now was if one of them was bleeding into the water.

Will tried to pull her up onto the wood. He got her up to her waist so only her legs dangled in the ocean. Then he lay his arms down and placed his head on them. The sun was beating down so furiously, his head was heating up to the point that it was causing vertigo.

"Have you ever been in love?" she said softly.

"Once. You?"

"I don't know." She paused. "You're the closest I've come."

He swallowed, the sensation one of dryness and scraping in his throat as though eating a cactus. "You're going to get married and have children. You'll be one of those old women with a good lifetime of memories behind you."

She smiled, her lips so cracked Will saw a slight tear when she did so. "I would like that... What was she like?"

"Who?"

"The woman you were in love with."

"Oh, her. I don't know, wild I guess. We met in Atlantic City. We gambled and drank that entire first night we met. Then we were inseparable for almost a month. I thought I was going to marry her. To bring her back to LA and settle down. And then one day she kissed me on the cheek, said thank you, and left. No rhyme or reason. She just saw men as playthings and when she grew bored she moved on."

"That's not love, silly. That's infatuation. If she had moved back to Los Angeles with you, you would have been the one to grow bored and leave her."

"Yeah, maybe."

She tilted her head upward, looking at the sky. The first real movement she'd had all day other than touching Will's fingers. "It'll be dark soon."

Will looked out over the water. "I know."

32

The sun dipped quickly. Or maybe it just seemed quick because he was watching it.

The glowing orb disappeared and left only its dim remnants in the sky, and even those faded away until nothing was left but darkness. A pure black that permeated everything around them.

By now, Will was shivering so much he couldn't keep his mouth closed. His teeth would tap against each other, creating a rapping sound in his head that was driving him crazy. The more he tried to stop it, the harder they tapped against each other. So he relaxed and let his body do whatever it was going to do.

"Listen to me," he said, the words coming through chattering teeth. "Whatever happens to me, you stay on this plank. Don't move from it to help me. I'll be fine."

She gripped his hand tighter. Will didn't have the strength to squeeze back, so he just closed his eyes.

The temperature at night dropped so fast he didn't even have time to be scared. The shivering reached a pitch where he wasn't sure he could hold on to the plank anymore. Elizabeth held his hand and that was the only thing keeping him there.

"If one of us has the chance to survive at the expense of the other," she said, "we have to take it. If you need to sacrifice me to live, don't hesitate, Will."

"No—no. I wo—won't."

"You have to. You have to live."

The blackness engulfed them until the moon revealed itself when the clouds slowly parted. The water was lit up a dim white. Like a ghost.

The shark activity had increased during the day and he could only guess what was going on at night. Underneath him in the murkiness, he saw the predators in his mind's eye. They were waiting for him to get weaker. They could sense death. He still could take out an eye, bash a nose or bite a fin. But soon he wouldn't even be able to do that. He would just be a passive slab of meat ready for the taking. And he pictured them knowing that.

A fin sliced through the water near him. This wasn't the small fin from before. This was large, maybe a foot, maybe more. And it moved with a casual grace that said this predator didn't have anything else in the ocean to fear.

The shark circled them and then disappeared again into the dark.

"Will, one of us has to live. If you can live, you take that chance."

"Wh—why are you saying all this? What does it matter?"

"It matters to me. It's the natural order. One of us has to survive... or else it wins."

The fin was back, the shark's crescent tail displacing

water as it came closer to the surface. The shark's frame came into view. It was a medium-sized fish, about nine or ten feet long with a massive head. Will knew he wasn't bleeding, but he had once heard that sharks could hear the heartbeats of prey in the water. How ironic that would be, he thought. That the thing that had given him breath every second of his life would be the thing to betray him and lead to his death.

The shark was getting closer. It was curious right now, still trying to figure out if what it was seeing was edible. In one pass, it came right up to Will, perhaps no more than a few inches behind him. Will screamed and pounded the fish on the snout.

The shark banked sharply to the left, surprised. But it didn't let up. It circled around wider and then tilted slightly to the right, swinging toward him like a fighter plane. It wasn't trying to hide its presence at all, and that's when Will knew it was over. When the fish understood that it had nothing to fear from him.

And just as the shark neared, its mouth open slightly, it quickly shot down into the dark. And suddenly the sea was quiet.

Will scanned the waters for any movement or fins, but there was nothing. The shark had simply disappeared.

Fear gripped his guts. His mind had shut off and the rational thinking that should have been rolling through him wasn't there. Just a cold, blank, primal fear. Something a lizard would feel upon knowing a superior predator was in the vicinity.

Will turned around, letting go of the plank a moment so he could see behind him. Nothing there. Just black ocean for as far as he could see.

“What?” Elizabeth asked.

“We—we’re either very lucky, or—or ver—very unlucky.”

33

The night dragged on with no commotion. Will had counted on attempting to fight off sharks the entire night, at least until his body gave out. But that hadn't happened. Instead, he was fighting the odd sensation of freezing to death.

He had once known a man that had been stranded in the arctic. David something or other. At a dinner party, he told everyone what freezing to death was like. It wasn't what you read about in papers or books. He described it as pure pain. A type of blinding pain that overtook every other sense and reduced a man to a babbling animal.

Then at the very end, heat. The body would heat itself up so high that the brain would boil in the skull. Many people in the arctic, this man assured everyone, had been found nude when they froze to death because they would strip themselves bare attempting to reduce the intense heat.

Will wasn't there yet. But the shivering was slowing. He didn't know what that meant because he was colder than ever. But whatever it meant, it couldn't have been good. It felt almost like his body giving up, against his spirit and his mind.

"My f—father once t—told me that it's good we don't l—live long. Because we—we'll always grow wic—wicked over time."

Elizabeth could hardly respond. It took her several inhalations of breath to work up enough power to say, "Your father sounds wise."

"He w—wasn't."

Will couldn't guess how much of the night was behind them or how much ahead of them, but he knew if he survived tonight, he would never take the sun for granted again. No matter how much it burned him.

A change in pressure occurred just underneath him. Something akin to a rising swell. The pressure was actually enough to lift Will out of the water before lowering him back down. Almost like something large passed by underneath him.

The water was so dark he couldn't see past the surface. And he didn't have the strength to curl his legs up to his chest and give whatever the hell passed underneath him a smaller area of attack. So he dangled there helplessly; like a leaf in the wind, he thought.

"I think... I think it followed us," he said.

The two of them didn't speak again for a long while. There was nothing left to say. Just an agonizing wait in the dark. Will tried to fill his mind with pleasant memories. Oddly, none of the ones he thought he would be having at this moment were there.

He thought he'd picture the drunken parties with the beautiful women hanging off his arm, or the luxurious hotels all over the world he would sleep in, or the fine clothes, wine and cars he would have at his disposal. He had an entire life of material excess and in this moment, when he wanted nothing more than to pull up a memory that would comfort him, none of those memories came.

The ones that came to him were about people. He thought of his mother and the way her arms would wrap all the way around his body and make him feel safe. He thought of his father and the time he took him fishing at a stream. They sat on the bank of the stream all day and didn't catch a single fish. But his father told him everything he knew about life. It was, as far as he could remember, the greatest day of Will's life.

But he also thought of Tyler, and of his business partner Cal, and of Elizabeth. When it counted, only memories of people came to him.

"Will..."

The voice was a whisper. If he hadn't been a couple of feet away from her, he wouldn't have heard it. He glanced up to her. Terror had gripped her features. It made her eyes widen and the only movement she made was to uncurl a single finger pointing in one direction. Will looked.

Something had broken the surface of the water. Something slick, something awful... The thing circled around until it landed on the wooden plank. It was about the thickness of an exhaust pipe and would alternate a deep red with a bright white color. Attached to the thing were suckers. Small circles with something inside. Will could see that what was held inside was even more terrifying than what was on the outside.

Hooks.

Something like claws, except that there were dozens of them because there were dozens of suckers.

A tentacle. Leading beneath the surface to something

Will could only imagine. The tentacle appeared like some giant tongue; slick, smelly and darting around.

"What is it?" she said.

"Shh..."

The tentacle explored the plank of wood, as though it were a child's hand gripping something new for the first time. As it crawled over the plank, it left slimy grease where it had been.

The tentacle reminded him of a snake, in that it could narrow itself and then expand again. But it was far more terrifying than any snake he'd ever seen. When it glowed red, it lit up the night around it. And when it faded to white, it was like some hand back from the grave, grasping for anything in sight to pull down to hell with it.

"Don't move," Will whispered.

The tentacle dipped below the water. Will didn't feel anything, any change in pressure. It was possible that it had left, believing that nothing but a piece of wood was there. But then, entirely in silence, it slid out of the water again, this time on the other side of the plank.

The tentacle ran down the wood again and came to Will. He closed his eyes. It ran over his back and his face. It felt like a wet honeydew melon smearing over him. It pulled away, and continued down the plank toward Elizabeth.

Slowly, Will opened his eyes and looked at her. Her hand was over her mouth and she was forcibly suppressing a scream as the tentacle went over her dress. It lifted it off her body with its stickiness, and then went down her leg.

The tentacle separated from her and stood rigid out of the water, growing in height as though whatever it was connected to was coming up to the surface. It towered over them and Will could feel Elizabeth trembling.

"You have to stop moving," he whispered.

The tentacle slithered back into the ocean and caught some of her dress on the way down. The dress tore, and Elizabeth let out an involuntary squeal and pulled away from it.

The tentacle froze, just completely froze in the water where it was. Then it reached back and swung forward with such violence, Will thought it might cut her in half. But instead it slapped down with a loud splash as it coiled around Elizabeth's calf.

She screamed as the tentacle looped and tore her flesh. Will leapt at her.

He got a good grip on her arm at the elbow and she held onto him with both hands as they were sucked underneath.

It happened so fast, he didn't even realize he was underwater. He felt a change in temperature and the sky and water spun. They were being pulled down into the depths.

Slowly, what came into view made Will's heart drop into his stomach.

Several glowing tentacles danced around them in the dark. Will followed them down with his eyes and saw what they were connected to. A mass of flesh that he couldn't make out, except for one globe-sized eyeball. The eyeball was so huge, he could see it just from the dim glow the creature's flesh gave off. And underneath the eye, the creature spread out all its tentacles and arms, revealing a massive beak: like some monster bird.

It pulled them down with such force, Will felt himself losing his grip on her. He reached into his pocket with his free hand and flipped open the knife. Pulling himself down onto her body, he stabbed into the tentacle and cut across. The flesh was soft, softer than human flesh even, and cut easy.

The creature screamed. It sounded like the scream of a cat that was in a lot of pain. High in pitch and rolling, so loud that it hurt his ears. But the thing let go and he kicked with everything he had.

Elizabeth was in shock, and a trail of blood behind her told him the wound was deep in her leg where the creature had held her. But he could worry about that when they got to the surface. The only thing that told him he was actually climbing up was the moon, the pure white orb that drew him near.

They broke the surface at the same time and gulped air. Will saw the plank about ten feet away. Laying on his back and pulling Elizabeth behind him, he kicked until his legs burned and his lungs felt like they were going to burst.

He wrapped his left arm around the plank and held them both up. She wasn't shivering; but in fact she was growing colder.

"Hey... hey, stay with me. Stay wi—"

The violence of the motion made his world spin. Will didn't know which way he was going and didn't know if he had been thrown out of the water or pulled under, so he just hung on. He held Elizabeth tightly with one arm, and the plank with the other.

An incredible force was pulling her out of his arms. He wrapped his hand under her breasts at the chest bone, but with one massive yank, she was ripped away. He managed to grab her arm and realized he was being pulled under again, right toward the monstrous beak. His other arm was still tightly wrapped around the plank and he felt like he was being torn in half as the plank submerged but fought to get to the surface again.

He couldn't hold on to both. He felt his fingers slipping and knew her arm would be torn away from him.

He closed his eyes and thought, *I'll die before I let you go.*

She was suddenly and violently ripped from him, and disappeared into the blackness as he shot back to the surface.

34

Will had an image in his mind and it wouldn't leave. He was sitting on the porch of their home, their small farm back in his true home. His mother had baked something—a pie—and brought out a slice for him.

She sat down next to him as he ate, the only sounds the metallic clink of the fork against the plate and the breeze rustling through the dense Aspen trees. Her fingers ran through his hair and gave him the pleasant tingling that only a mother's touch can give. She kissed him on the forehead and said, "One day you'll be a great man. I knew it from the moment you were born. You were sick when you were young. They thought you couldn't breathe because your lungs weren't completely formed. And you fought so hard. I know you'll fight that hard in everything you do, Will. Always fight hard for what you want."

His mother. The images flooded his mind as though they were being poured in. He remembered the last time he saw her, weak and in a bed. Barely able to keep her eyes open. She took his hand and gave him a feeble smile...

much as Elizabeth had the last time they spoke.

Elizabeth.

The thought of her brought all the memories flooding back and he knew he had been unconscious, though he couldn't tell how long. But when he opened his eyes, he was cradling the plank of wood, slowly drifting on the ocean. The sun was up now and it warmed his face. He had just enough strength to lift his head and search around him. He was alone.

The events of the previous night were like something out of nightmares that the sunlight burned away. And just like a nightmare, he questioned whether it had actually happened. Or was this all a figment of his weakened state? His mind playing out entire scenarios as it lost grip with reality.

But the cold was something he knew he couldn't imagine. His body felt like ice and he had stopped shivering. No matter how violently his body shivered for warmth, it didn't frighten him. Now that it had stopped, the fear of death gripped him. It was when his body gave up that he knew his spirit would soon follow.

"Last day on earth," he mumbled weakly to himself, "and not a drink in sight."

He lay on the plank and drifted. Occasionally, he would hear splashing nearby. Perhaps a shark, perhaps not. Didn't matter. He couldn't fight them off. So he didn't pay any attention to them.

The heat was blistering now. And overhead, he heard something. A cawing. His eyes rolled up and he saw the sky, a clear blue sky with no clouds, the white frame of a seagull passing by overhead. He had heard somewhere that sailors considered them good omens and he smirked. "Ain't it just like me to go and die with a good omen right above," he whispered to himself.

The talking helped. Just hearing a voice, even if it was his own, helped. Eased the burden of solitude.

His nostrils caught a scent.

The ocean breeze had a distinct smell. Salty and somewhat putrid, like rotting seaweed. He detected a different scent now. It was almost like... land. A land scent. Woods and sand...

Will looked to the water. The deep blue he had grown accustomed to was now turning something else. A light green.

If he had had the strength to kick, he would have. But he didn't. And all he could do was hang on to the plank and hope that he was headed toward land rather than away from it.

Soon, the water grew muddy and he saw foliage. Large leaves that had long ago yellowed and died, bits of driftwood and long grass. He kept his eyes open, but every ounce of him was screaming for his eyes to close. To just fall into a dreamless sleep... and whether he woke up or not would be out of his hands.

He could see what appeared to be a low hanging cloud, white and puffy. As he drifted toward it, he could make out the contours of land. He thought maybe people were there on the beach but it was so far away he couldn't tell. "Please help," he mumbled, not loud enough for anyone to hear.

The excitement he felt was in his bones. A deep excitement that couldn't express itself because it was too profound. He was afraid to express it anyway. To even put into words that this ordeal might be over. Because he was afraid that what he was seeing wasn't real. That he would close his eyes and open them again only to find that it was just a cloud after all.

His eyes strained as he was unwilling to close them. Even blinking brought a terror with it that the land would disappear. But as he drifted close, he could see a long, flat beach. Small bumps were behind it and he thought of turtle shells. But they were sand dunes. And on the beach, he saw several people. He saw other things as well.

He saw trains and cars, girls in bathing suits that roughhoused with men and fumbled with each other in the surf. He saw children playing and dogs running around with them. It brought a smile to his face… and then he blinked, and it was gone. And the only thing before him was a desolate beach.

The water near the beach was choppy. It would foam as the swells hit the shore, rumbling from the impact.

Will realized there was no way for him to get in. The water was too violent, and he couldn't swim through the surf. "How funny," he said breathlessly, his eyes closed, "if I died with land right in front of me."

He drifted parallel to the shore, never really advancing. Sometimes he saw people, sometimes he saw entire buildings. Entire cities. But none of it was real. Or at least he didn't know if it was. One thing that he thought was real was the foliage he was seeing in the water. But even that seemed to drift past so quickly he couldn't be sure if it was really there or not.

He drifted for a long time. Just out of reach of the land that would save his life. His body felt like it wasn't there, or at least wasn't a part of him. Detached. Like his consciousness was a floating spirit watching everything from above. With land right there, his life in the balance, he could do nothing but close his eyes, and let the darkness take him.

35

When Bixby stepped off the ship onto land for the first time, it felt as though he had been granted some great gift by the universe. This morning, he had been given a meal of bacon and eggs, plums, and four pears. He'd wolfed it all down and finished it with a pint of beer.

The morning sun was bright as he stepped on to the port. He was back on English soil. Back home. Things like this were always imagined by seamen, but none of them ever thought it would happen to them. They couldn't think that. Because then going to sea would be impossible. He knew what their work really entailed. He went out sea, and knew that some people would die. He just took his chances that it wouldn't be him.

He was swamped with reporters, but he had no words for them. No great story. Not yet. He hadn't worked out what he would be telling the press. Whatever it was, men disappearing off the ship wouldn't be part of it. Unless of course that Yank was to blame. Maybe he had been the one throwing them off and Bixby made a valiant effort to save as many of the men as he could?

A car was waiting for him. He shuffled himself in. The driver turned the engine and pulled away. Bixby watched the reporters a while before the car passed them and went over a bridge. He kept his eyes on the sea. That damned sea that would never let him go.

When he was a child, he sat in a boat with his father, a degenerate drunk and gambler that would occasionally be inspired to try to parent. He grabbed Bixby under the arms and tossed him into the freezing sea. The boy couldn't swim, had never even been shown how. And now he was fighting for his life.

His father was yelling at him, "Get yer arse to the boat, boy!"

Bixby went under. He remembered the sensation of the ice-cold water covering his head like a waterfall.

He should have run as far inland as he could get and never looked back. But somehow, the sea would always pull him back.

"Good to have you home, Lieutenant," the driver said. "You've been in all the papers you know. They're saying you're a hero."

Bixby kept his eyes to the sea. "They can go to hell for all I care."

As the car turned a corner, the sea disappeared and was out of view. Bixby closed his eyes, and leaned his head back on the seat, a grin coming over his lips.

36

Will's eyes flitted open. A vibration was in the water. A soft hum. He gripped the plank tightly with both arms and heard himself say, "No!"

He kept his eyes on the water around him but didn't see anything. His vision was blurred, almost clouded over. So he closed his eyes.

The strength he'd had in his arms was long gone. He was holding on with vapors of strength that quickly faded away, and his grip loosened. Slowly, he began sinking into the water.

The sea covered him up, swallowed him, surrounded him on all sides. His eyes were open and he could see the sunlight, the last thing he would ever see. The sun was bright and appeared wavy from underneath the surface. The ocean was still today, few waves and even less movement. But that vibration was there, growing louder, getting nearer.

The water faded from greenish-blue to black, and just as the blackness was about to take him, he felt pressure on his arm. The thing had him.

He was thrust up through the surface and into the sunlight. Another sound was there... voices. The voices of men that gripped him and pulled him up onto a small boat. They weren't speaking English and they kept asking him questions he didn't understand. One man wrapped him in a blanket and the warmth was like a shock. Another had a thermos with something hot, coffee or tea or something similar. He drank some and it soothed his throat which felt like the desert floor without rain.

The boat was moving. He didn't know the direction it was going, and he hoped land rather than a larger vessel farther out to sea.

Soon, they were at a dock and the boat stopped. Two men with dark skin put each of his arms over their shoulders and lifted him up onto a pier. They were speaking quickly. A language he didn't recognize but that sounded vaguely of Spanish.

Farther up the pier, he could see a crowd of people staring at him. Will, unable to move anything but his eyes, looked at the water as he was taken off the pier, and onto dry land.

The following few hours were a flurry of movement. A cart pulled by a horse, a bumpy road. Something that resembled a hospital with a doctor peering into his eyes with a light. Injections in his arms and a soft bed. Sores on his legs and buttocks were cleaned and bandaged. No pain medication was given him and he didn't have the strength to speak, so he had to bear the pain.

But most of all, he felt warmth. The warmth of dry

clothes and a bed with sheets. He had never felt so warm in his life, and as if by magic, as the warmth flowed into him, so did life.

One woman, a nurse he guessed, came by later in the day, or possibly another day altogether. He couldn't tell. She had a kindly smile and legs that were revealed by a skirt. She softly touched his hand and spoke in that language he couldn't understand. Will got the impression she was trying to gather some sort of information.

"Thank you," was all he said, his eyes closing again. "Thank you."

37

Will Curtis smoked his cigar in the hallway. The building was lovely, one of the nicest he'd been to in London. The interior was all wood paneling and green plants. Persian rugs were on the floor and the elevator doors were trimmed with freshly cleaned brass.

A newspaper was out on one of the fine antique chairs. He had grown quite sick of newspapers.

The first article he'd read about the *Britannia* didn't even mention him. One of the other lifeboats was filled with over fifty men and most of them survived. They took up most of the space on the printed page.

Another lifeboat contained a woman of substantial means and she had published her story in the *New York Magazine* and a few other places. She was causing quite the stir as a socialite and would go on a speaking tour at universities and talk about survival and holding on to your virtue in such a situation. Will knew the account of both those people's lifeboats. They were rescued quickly by British ships, none of them on the water longer than a day or two.

The first article to mention him was in an English newspaper. They quoted him as saying that he believed people had been disappearing off their lifeboat. And the culprit was later "revealed" to him to be a "monster of such enormous proportions that only the Greeks of old could account for it."

Of course, there was no evidence of this, the paper continued. And in fact, the other survivor of the lifeboat, one Lieutenant Kyle Bixby, contradicted this account and said that it was Mr. Will Curtis himself who was throwing the weak and the sick overboard to make the rations last longer.

After that, Will never read the papers again. Or any accounts of what had occurred on the *Britannia* or its lifeboats.

At night, he was usually occupied by nightmares. A glowing beak in darkness, flashing red flesh all around him as Elizabeth's milk-white face haunted him. Screamed to him.

The nightmares had subsided of late. But he couldn't do what he did before. The parlors of the wealthy where he mingled and played no longer held any luster for him. The embrace of buxom women felt cold against his skin. And making money seemed about as trivial a thing as he could think to do.

So he'd gotten rid of all of it. A piece of land on the Montana border had cost him a fraction of the money he received when Cal had bought out his half of the business. On that land, he saw a family. Children running around squealing, the sound of dogs barking playfully... and a wife. Someone pure and innocent. Someone that the heartache of life didn't affect.

He knew now what lesson he'd learned on the ocean:

life was about survival, but it was a chosen survival. And if you chose to live, if you chose to try, you had to go all the way. No half-measures, no dreaming of tomorrow. No pondering the way it ought to be. You had to go all the way, or not even bother.

And he'd gone all the way. He sold every possession he'd owned and bought a piece of land with a cabin being built on it. He would have his food, his clothes, and a bloodhound he'd bought from a neighboring farm. All of that was waiting for him back in the wide-open plains of his own property. But he had to take care of one thing first.

The large man ambled through the front doors of the building. He glanced over and noticed Will but didn't take him into account until he was almost to the elevator. There, he stopped and slowly turned to face him.

"Hello, Bixby," Will said, sucking on the cigar.

Bixby smirked. "I wondered if you'd ever come lookin' for me."

"Well, now you have your answer."

Bixby stepped closer to him. "Shame 'bout that girl dyin'. I did like her."

"You sentenced her to death. Her, and me, and my friend Tyler."

He shrugged. "So? What're you gonna do 'bout it?"

Will lowered the cigar. "I've thought about that a lot. See, I heard how you told them there were no survivors. They called off the search parties after that. So I wondered if she and my friend would be alive right now if it wasn't for you."

Bixby was silent a moment. "They mock you in the papers, but I believed your story. A red tentacled monster. The Kraken," he said with a smile. "Like I said, I believe, but it does sound rather ridiculous. Him slowly hunting us and pulling people off the boat at night. It's just a dumb animal. It don't think like that."

Will was silent a moment. "You didn't see it. It was like the gates'a hell opened up and there it was, staring back at me."

Bixby glanced out the door, either to make sure no one was coming in, or to see if he could make it out in time. Will couldn't tell which.

"So," Bixby said, "what did you decide? That I needed to die?"

He shook his head. "No. I think I've had enough death. I could kill you right now if I wanted, but I'm not going to. But I wanted to tell you that to your face. Tell you I ain't scared of you anymore, and I'm choosing to let you live."

Bixby reached his hand behind him. "You know, I never did get my knife back. That's my favorite knife."

The two men didn't move. Will let the cigar dangle in his fingers. Slowly, he brought it up to his lips. Right when the cigar touched, he pulled, lighting the tip red. Bixby smiled... and made his move.

The revolver came out of nowhere. Bixby lifted and fired one round that went wide, scraping Will's shoulder. The small pistol in Will's holster on his hip came up. He didn't have time to withdraw it so he bent the holster up and fired through it.

The first round missed but the second went into Bixby's chest. The big man took one step back, but no more. The smell of gunpowder filled the lobby and Will's ears were ringing. The two of them stood for a long time, long enough that the ringing in his ears stopped. A small trickle of blood rolled down Bixby's shirt, appearing as a wet stain from his chest to his belly.

The big man fell to his knees, clutching his handgun. He toppled over with his eyes to the ceiling, his light slowly dimming. Will pulled a knife from his pocket. The same knife that he'd tried to save Elizabeth with. And, briefly, he wondered if he'd come here to kill Bixby. Knowing the big man would try to kill him first and one of them would have to die. But it was a question that, ultimately, didn't matter. Fate had decreed that one of them had to end up like this. With their eyes to the ceiling as the life drained from them.

He tossed the knife on the big man's chest and walked out.

EPILOGUE

Several children ran on the grass as the two bloodhounds chased them. Good dogs, dogs bred for life on a ranch. As their parents had been. Will Curtis watched the dogs as he sipped a drink in a tumbler. His children, three boys, ran around like they had all the time and energy in the world. And there was nothing in the world he loved more than to sit out here and watch them.

He glanced back through the window and saw his wife, Jasmine, cooking something on the stove. He caught a glimpse of his reflection. His hair had gone gray at the temples and he had wrinkles near the eyes. Jasmine said they were experience wrinkles and assured him they were more manly than the smooth baby-face he'd had when they'd first met.

His wife came out and leaned against the doorframe of their home. She watched the boys with an odd mixture of adoration and fear. Adoration because there was no one on earth she felt closer to, and fear because she didn't want them to go out into the world yet.

"I hope we can teach them right," she said, in her thick Montana small-town speech.

"They're good boys. They'll learn what they need to learn."

"You're a good father."

He finished the drink in the tumbler and said, "Boys, come here." The boys stopped playing and came up to the porch. The oldest, Tyler, leaned against the post, but the two younger ones, Martin and Will Junior sat down.

"You boys are old enough to hear a story now that I've been wanting to tell you." He hesitated. "But before I tell you this story, I want you to make me a promise. Promise me you'll all follow your hearts. Forget about clearing your minds, clear your hearts. And then follow them into what you love. 'Cause if you don't, you're going to end up in a place you don't want to be." Will took a deep breath and then said, "It was about twenty years ago that I lived in Los Angeles..."

48061692R00117

Printed in Poland
by Amazon Fulfillment
Poland Sp. z o.o., Wrocław